Feeling It

A Novel

Hank Whittemore

Forever Press
2016

ISBN 978-0-9835027-8-4

Published by

Forever Press
PO Box 263
Somerville, MA 02143
www.foreverpress.org

Cover design by Forever Press
With contributions from Katherine Potter,
Joe Gorelick and William Boyle

Cover Images, Clockwise:

Laurence Olivier in *Hamlet* (1948); Dodgers:
John Jorgensen, Pee Wee Reese, Ed Stanky &
Jackie Robinson (1947); James Dean in *Rebel
Without a Cause* (1955); The Author on his
Go-Kart, back in the day

Oliver, Dean and Dodgers images courtesy of Wikimedia Commons

Printed in the USA

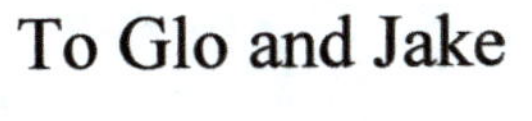

To Glo and Jake

Dear Reader:

I wrote this novel in 1970, when I was turning twenty-nine, and it was published by William Morrow and Company the following year. The book was my first novel and was accepted as an Alternate Selection of the Literary Guild of America. In addition to the book's warm reception by many readers, it holds a special place in my author's heart, so I'm happy to be able to share it again with a new audience.

I have always been grateful for the guidance of James Landis, editor of the book at Morrow. The text in this edition is unchanged except for an added Table of Contents with titled chapters.

There is an autobiographical basis for the time frame and physical settings of *Feeling It*, but the characters and story are fictional. Any resemblance to persons living or dead is coincidental.

Thanks to Katherine Potter and Joe Gorelick for their expertise and help with the cover design, and to William Boyle for his publishing skills. Ultimately the responsibility for any aspect of this book is mine alone.

Hank Whittemore
Nyack, New York
2016

About the author

Hank Whittemore grew up in Larchmont, NY and graduated from Mamaroneck High School and the university of Notre Dame. He has been an actor, newspaper reporter and radio news announcer. He has written ten books issued by mainstream publishers and several others about Edward de Vere, Earl of Oxford and the Shakespeare authorship question. He has written dozens of scripts for documentary film and television, and about a hundred feature articles for PARADE, the Sunday supplement. With Ted Story he wrote a 90-minute one-man show, *Shake-speare's Treason*, which Hank has performed around the country and in England. Books by L.H. (Hank) Whittemore:

The Man Who Ran the Subways: The Story of Mike Quill (Holt, 1968)
Cop! A Closeup of Violence and Tragedy – (Holt, 1969)
Feeling It – A Novel (Morrow, 1971)
Together: A Reporter's Journey into the New Black Politics (Morrow, 1971)
The Super Cops: The True Story of the Cops Called Batman and Robin (Stein & Day, 1973)
Peroff: The Man Who Knew Too Much (Morrow, 1974)
Find the Magician! The Counterfeiting Crime of the Century (Viking, 1979)
CNN: The Inside Story: How a Band of Mavericks Changed the Face of TV News (Little, Brown, 1990)
So That Others May Live: Caroline Hebard and Her Search-and-Rescue Dogs (Bantam, 1994)
Your Future Self: A Journey to the Frontiers of Molecular Medicine (Thames &Hudson, 1998)
The Monument: "Shake-Speares Sonnets" by Edward de Vere, 17th Earl of Oxford (Meadow Geese, 2005)
Twelve Years in the Life of Shakespeare (Forever Press, 2012)

Table of Contents

1

Eddie and Me

After the war, my father came home and went into the field of advertising. He rose through the corporate ranks, so to speak, and we bought a house in the Village of Bushmont, only an hour's drive from New York City. We lived on East Valley Stream Road, which ran parallel to West Valley Stream Road. Running between the two streets was a rather large brook, which babbled in the spring, stagnated in the summer, and froze in the winter. We moved there in the month of July, and within the first week I met my best friend, Eddie Reilly.

The first time I saw him he was hanging upside down from a tree outside our kitchen window. I was eating breakfast with my parents, when I looked up and saw this smiling, upside-down face in the window. My mother screamed, and my father and I ran out the back door. When we got to the tree, Eddie was gone.

The next time I saw him he was squatting at the edge of the brook, his forehead resting on his knees. I walked over to him and said, "What's the matter?"

Eddie looked up at me and pointed to a dead sunfish that was lying in the grass beside him. I glanced at the fish, but failed to see what the big problem was. As a matter of fact, I had seen that very fish only a few hours before. It had been floating on its side near the center of the brook, and I had walked right by it with hardly a thought.

"By the way," I said, "my name's David Marsh."

"Yeah. I saw you eating breakfast the other day."

"What were you doing, hanging from that tree branch?"

"Eh."

"What's your name?"

But Eddie Reilly's mind was somewhere else.

Bushmont Village was full of trees and distinctive homes. A perfect location, as they say. Excellent neighborhood! Near schools and houses of worship! Buy now! Only $97,500—a *steal* in today's market. Maid's room, eat-in kitchen, *two powder rooms!* FAIRYTALE SETTING! A bedroom community with class! The only thing the advertisements didn't tell you was that Bushmont Village, by some incredible trick of the zoners' pencils, was right next to a sprawling Negro slum. Well, not really next to it, but *overlooking* it. And I suppose it wasn't a *sprawling* slum, either; but it was, definitely, a slum. The classified ads didn't say that Bushmont was part of the Town of Brookdale. The Village had its own government and police force and train station, but still it remained, structurally and geographically, part of the town. At one edge of Bushmont was a cliff from which you could look down and see the "old downtown" of Brookdale, known as the Flats. BRILLIANT VIEW OF SEETHING SLUMS! That's where Ella Washington, our maid, lived. I used to imagine her scaling the walls of the cliff from the Flats up to Bushmont, in order to get to our house. Otherwise, for me, the Flats might have been a thousand miles away.

The kids on Valley Stream Road used to brag about their fathers a lot. One exception, though, was Kenny Starro, whose dad was a raving drunk and probably a madman. One time he tied Kenny's mother to the piano seat in their living room, sat on her, and played the National Anthem for three straight hours while she screamed and Kenny pissed in his pants in the corner. True! His father went on periodic binges that lasted about a week at a time. Otherwise, you would have thought everything was normal.

Anyway, the Valley Stream Stinkers (Eddie's name for us) used to argue for hours on end over whose dad made the most money, or owned the best car, or had the finest record of action in the war. None of us knew how much our fathers made, so that kind of debate could go on for at least a whole summer.

Joyce Clarkson, for example, used to brag about how her father was second only to the President. Her old man was a big shot with some TV network, and his promotions received very good coverage in *The New York Times*. Joyce, whose long blond hair seemed to lend authority to her words, would tell us all about how her father had helped to get General Eisenhower elected President.

"He didn't do any such thing," said Eddie Reilly, our leader. "Eisenhower was a *general*. He was a *war hero*, Joyce. So your father couldn't have had anything to *do* with his getting elected."

"You don't know anything!" Joyce answered. She could get about as angry as any little girl you'd want to know. She was always taking dancing lessons and practicing her figure skating and riding horseback. In fact, she gave the impression, when she was talking to you, or *at* you, that she was *still* looking down from the saddle of a horse.

As for the war records, it was a matter of whose old man, or which kid, had the wildest imagination. For example, Neil Ulrich swore up and down that his father's plane had been shot down in the middle of the ocean, and that he swam back to shore.

Eddie's father had Parkinson's disease or multiple sclerosis, I was never sure which. Dr. Reilly had been unable to serve in the military, so Eddie couldn't participate in the war-record debates. In fact, he never bragged about his father at all, because he didn't need to. We all knew that Dr. Reilly was a great man, since he had forced himself to continue as a general practitioner despite his terrible illness.

My dad didn't fare too well in the "great war tales" category, although I was in there plugging for him. I used to ask him about the Army, about his exploits, so I could relay them back to the Stinkers; but the only salvageable piece of information I got from him was that one time he went into the woods somewhere in Europe, to take a crap, and heard the sound of a sniper's bullet.

"How close did the bullet come to you, Dad?"

"Oh, about fifty yards."

Now, in those days I thought that "yards" meant backyards, and with the substantial lawns in Bushmont for a reference, fifty of them sounded like a mile and a half. But I persisted.

"Were you afraid, Dad?"

"Of course, David."

"Did the bullet ricochet off a tree or anything?"

"No, son."

"Was there a chance it might have really hit you?"

"I don't think so. Well, of course there was a *chance*. Certainly. But I was crouching down, going to the bathroom, so I had plenty of cover."

A pretty weak tale of heroism to bring back to the Valley Stream Stinkers. I worked it over in my mind before retelling it to them. By the time I got around to bringing it up, I had inflated my father's story to the point where I pictured him squatting in the thicket, calmly taking a crap, "when suddenly a hail of bullets and grenades burst through the trees." With all eyes following me, I told of my father, pants down around his ankles, splattering five oncoming Nazis with his machine gun.

Eddie Reilly had a number of good laughs over that one. He never believed me for a minute. When Eddie thought something was funny, he'd laugh about it for weeks. He was a stocky little Irish kid with a contagious giggle. I thought he'd never quit chuckling over that story I made up about my father. We'd be playing some kind of game, either in his house or in his backyard or in the street, and right out of the blue he'd squat down, pretending to be my father taking a crap. Then he'd make like he was firing the machine gun and the next moment he'd fall over laughing in that high-pitched voice of his and holding his sides. I couldn't get angry with him, because pretty soon he'd have me laughing, too.

"Private Marsh," he'd say, referring to my father and nearly crying with laughter, "honored for bravery while defending his pile of shit."

I suppose it was natural for us to compare notes. Adults do it all the time, but in more subtle ways. Kids argue openly about status, with no worry over tact. "My old man makes at *least* a hundred grand," I'd say. "Whaddya got that station wagon for, then? It's a *year old.*" "We happen to *like* our car, that's why." But for all our bragging and competing, some of which must have come from our parents themselves, we shared a vague sadness over our fathers' lives. I used to talk about this with Eddie. He and I would sit on his back steps munching apples and discuss what we wanted to be when we grew up. I never knew what in hell I wanted to be, but Eddie always had a different idea, like being a forest ranger or a ship's captain or an airline pilot or an "explorer" of some kind.

"What I *don't* want to do," he would say, "is commute to New York every day. Imagine that? Every morning, the same train. And the same one every evening. And sitting at the same desk for eight hours a day! Wearing the same kind of clothes all the time! Always a tiel I'd go nuts. Absolutely nuts!"

"Me too, Ed."

"With two lousy weeks of vacation every year."

"My father gets three weeks now,"' I offered.

"What's the difference? Imagine *having* to go to work, or even to take a vacation, even when you didn't *want* to? I mean, school is bad enough. We'll be nearly eighteen by the time we get out of school. Think of what we gotta go through —junior high, that'll be three years, and senior high, that's another three. I *know* I won't want to go to college. And I certainly won't become a commuter."

"Ah, I bet you will, Ed. You'll at least go to college."

"No, I won't."

"What'll you do?"

"I dunno. But I'm not gonna commute. I'm not even gonna live in Bushmont. And I'm gonna stay outdoors as much as I can. Maybe even *live* outdoors. I could live off the land."

"Why won't you live in Bushmont?"

"David, we'll have lived here for most of our lives! Can you imagine becoming old and buying a house *right next door* to where you grew up? Or in the same town? Oh, man, that would be terrible!"

It was about this time when I perceived something of our predicament. Bushmont was a nice little village, but it was *too* nice, really. It was a place into which you might graduate, so to speak, rather than a place to grow up in. Our fathers had struggled to gain their patches of ground in Bushmont, but what incentive did we have, since we were already there?

Like most of the kids in our neighborhood, I may have had these thoughts, but I couldn't find ways to express them. Most likely we were just too lazy to do anything other than what seemed to be expected of us. The only one who possessed the necessary creative imagination was Eddie Reilly. Everybody, including me, would wander over to Eddie's backyard and say, "Whaddya wanna do today, Ed?"

And Eddie would sit there with his little sailor hat tipped back and reply, "I dunno. Wadda-*you* wanna do?"

"I dunno."

This would go on for about twenty minutes, while we waited for Eddie to make the first move. We knew that soon he'd get to his feet without saying a word and begin some brand-new adventure for the day. He avoided all forms of regulated or organized activity, such as playing basketball or Monopoly or Ping-Pong, and he hardly ever went swimming at the Bushmont Beach and Yacht Club. Eddie's games were all initiated within his own head. On different occasions he had us build birdhouses and sell them door-to-door, create a carnival in his backyard, make underground forts in the "hidden hay field" in the woods, build a raft to float on the brook, catch turtles in the Duck Pond, construct a wooden fort in his willow tree, set up walkie-talkies between our houses, and on and on.

One of the best Eddie-inspired adventures occurred one summer night when he had us take off all our clothes and sneak into the village shopping district (about a mile) and back again without being seen. This feat required a great amount of ingenuity, since we had to hide behind rocks and trees and garages and to sprint from one place of concealment to another. Imagine spotting four naked boys and one girl in a slip dashing across your backyard and over the fence!

There was a fundamental difference between the way Eddie coped with our comfortable environment and the way we did. Whereas we just slipped into the patterns that were set up for us, Eddie was able to stand outside them; and he was able to *use* them, to mold his environment according to his own imagination. For example, the act of running naked through backyards and across streets—right into town!—transformed Bushmont, for us, into an alien territory in which at any moment we might have been caught. Crouching behind a car in someone's driveway with our clothes off, we were compelled to look at the slightest movements—of other people, of cars, of lights being switched on and off—in a completely new context. For a glorious two hours or so we lived as though we were fugitives from our own community, yet it was that very community which gave us such security and casual confidence in the future.

My hat was off to Eddie Reilly, who for so many brief but wonderful moments was able to turn our lives, and our relationship to everything around us, inside out. Running naked, we were fugitives; selling birdhouses, we became, not kids, but *real salesmen;* the carnival turned Eddie's backyard into an exotic land in which *we were the exotic people* whom our parents and other dull neighbors came to gawk at; the underground forts transformed the woods into an island of dark legends and secrets, a strange land in which *we were the natives, the strange people;* and so on, all thanks to Eddie and his unstoppable, unrivaled imagination.

Yet there was an aura of loneliness about Eddie, a

kind of sadness. How long could he keep up this stuff? Wouldn't the time come when he'd have to temper his imagination and start dealing with reality? Most of us sensed this. We encouraged Eddie, we followed him in each new inspired escapade, but at the same time we slowly, steadily backed away from him in our minds, telling ourselves that there were also *important* things to be considering.

The time crept up when all of us kids were viewing Eddie Reilly as if from the outside, from a distance. We were still playing with him as his friend, but a subtle, intangible change was taking place. Kenny was now talking about how he wanted to become either a priest or a dancer. Little Artie was getting high grades in arithmetic and saying, "My folks think I ought to become an engineer."

"What's an engineer?"

"I don't really know. Something about building bridges and buildings. But it helps if you do good in math."

Neil Ulrich was now talking about how some girl had taken his hand (at age twelve?) and had put it under her dress. And I was thinking about playing baseball in the Little League. Suddenly we were competing, whether we knew it or not, for grades and girls and positions on organized teams, and against each other. Grades, girls, and organized sports: these were the subjects which brought forth groans of disdain from Eddie Reilly. They required no imagination. They were just there, like hors d'oeuvres passed around on a tray. To take one was to lose one's grip on freedom. In school, Eddie would seize any opportunity to break out of its clutches. He set up a secret gambling concession in the Boys' Room, he was always asking me to gyp school to spend the day in the woods, and in class he seemed to *deliberately* flunk tests (after all, wasn't he the most ingenious kid I knew?). At parties, Eddie would never play Spin the Bottle or any other game; he would sit in the corner all night, occasionally mocking the guys who were bold enough to ask a girl to dance.

Even as I'm recalling this I can feel a certain tendency on my part to portray Eddie as a deadbeat, and that's a shame because he was just the *opposite* from a deadbeat. He was more alive than any of us. Yet because he refused to join, because he didn't *need* to join, he slowly was pushed to the background.

I didn't know whether the other kids had these thoughts, but I certainly did; maybe because Eddie was such a good friend of mine. He would call me up and I'd say, "Hello?"

"Hi, it's Ed."

"Hi, Eddie."

"What do you want, David?"

"Eddie, *you* called *me*."

"Well, what do you want?"

"Come on, Ed. I don't want anything."

"You must want *something.*"

I couldn't think of anything, so Eddie would hang up.

Toward the end of the summer before we went on to the seventh grade, Eddie and I were skipping flat rocks on the brook when he abruptly said, "Let's go."

"Where?"

"Anywhere. Everywhere."

"What do you mean, Ed?"

"Let's just leave. We'll hitchhike to a train and then to the ocean, the Pacific, so we get a chance to go across the country first, and then we'll take a boat to China. We'll just keep going. Around the world, anywhere we feel like. Everywhere. Just keep moving, wherever things take us. All our lives."

"*All our lives!*"

"Sure. Why not?"

"Why not!"

"Yeah, why not?"

"Jeez, Ed, there's a million reasons why not."

"Tell me one."

"What about our families?"

"What about 'em?"

"They'd *miss* us," I said.

"We could pass through Bushmont every once in a while, every year or two, and say hello."

"What about money?"

"What about it?"

"Eddie, things cost money. Like trains or boats. And food."

"We could stow away. Or even *work* our way around the world."

Eddie and I fell silent. We skipped a few more rocks and he said, "So we'll go away, okay?"

"When?"

"Tomorrow night."

"*Tomorrow night!*"

"Sure. Why not? Why wait?"

"Well, man, Ed . . ."

"We'll leave at midnight, at the bridge."

He was talking about the bridge at the end of Valley Stream Road, where another street crossed over the brook. We didn't say anything more about going away until next afternoon. Eddie was in his garage, trying to attach a lawn mower engine to an old pushcart he had made. He looked up at me and said, "Tonight. Twelve o'clock at the bridge. By this time tomorrow we'll be gone. Right?"

"Right."

Of course I didn't think he was serious, yet I knew he was *deadly* serious. He started telling me what to bring in my knapsack and advised me to write a polite note to my parents and to leave it for them on my kitchen table. I was beginning to get extremely nervous.

"Eddie," I said, "let's not go tonight. Let's wait a while."

"Why? You afraid?"

"No, of course not."

"So what do you wanna wait for?"

"I don't know. I just . . ."

"Give me one good reason why we shouldn't go right away."

"Eddie, I'm wondering if we should go at all."

"Give me one good reason why not."

"I can't, but . . ."

There were a million reasons, of course, but none that I could give to Eddie. There was school. We'd be left behind! And if we were left behind in school, we'd fall behind all our friends, and. . . . But Eddie would have laughed at that reason for not going. He would have replied, "It doesn't matter, because we *couldn't* be left behind. If we're *never coming back,* except to visit, how could we be left behind?" And he would have been right, too, since it's impossible to lose a race that you never enter.

So I wasn't able to argue with him. To have stated flatly that I wasn't going with him would have been to have admitted, openly, that I had chosen the easy, boring road in life. I might as well have said that I'd probably become a commuter! As I left for home that evening, he yelled, "Remember, Dave—midnight at the bridge! By tomorrow we'll be gone!"

"Right, Ed. Midnight."

During dinner with my folks I noticed everything — their faces, their voices, their mannerisms — as if it were the Last Supper. I went to my room and lay down on my bed, trying to think of what it would be like to travel around the world, *endlessly*, with Eddie Reilly. And suddenly I became terrified. It occurred to me that by the age of twenty-one I'd be a poor bum stranded somewhere, and that if something happened to Eddie I'd be left alone without anything.

And lying there on my bed, thinking about going away with Eddie, I started to panic. I wanted to call him up and just say, "Ed, I'm not going." But I was also afraid to do that. I couldn't bear to face his reaction, even over the phone.

At eleven o'clock I turned off my light and got under the covers with my clothes on. My mother came upstairs and kissed me goodnight, and I told her to shut the door behind her "to keep out the light." At midnight I was feeling so nervous and guilty that I slipped out of bed, went through my closet and snuck out the window onto the roof. I climbed down our stone chimney and hopped over the backyard fence to Neil's yard. Then I shinnied up a drain pipe to the top of his garage. I crawled to where I could look down, across the side yard and the road, to the bridge. What a relief to see nothing but shadows of bushes and trees, to hear nothing but the faint gurgling of the brook.

Then from around the corner came the familiar footsteps of Eddie Reilly. He looked like he had *already* been around the world as he approached the bridge with a duffel bag over his shoulder. He sat down quietly on the wall that bordered the brook, as if to rest, and his shadow spread across the road under the streetlight. He held his knees up to his chest and leaned calmly against the bag in the dark.

He was waiting for me. I don't think that I really had expected him to show up. Somewhere in the back of my mind I had been hoping that "going away" would prove to be just a fantasy that Eddie had dreamed up, perhaps to test me or even to play a joke. But there he was, waiting for me, apparently dead-serious about the whole thing.

I must have stayed on that garage roof for at least thirty minutes, watching my best friend and wishing that I'd have the guts to join him. I was also wishing that Eddie would pick up his duffel bag and go back home. Then the next day I'd make up some excuse about my parents catching me or something.

All of a sudden Eddie began to whistle. He let out his crow call, which sounded exactly like a crow. Then he resumed the whistling. God, would he stay there *all night?*

How much trust in me did he have? Had he seen, in me, a spirit like his own?

In the silence, in my silence, I wondered what was going through his mind. Thinking that I had probably lost my best friend forever, I started crying for the first time since I was a tiny child. I kept an arm over my sobbing mouth and nose, but the tears streamed down.

When I looked up again, Eddie was standing on the wall with a coil of rope in his hand. He was throwing it over a tree branch that hung across the brook. He threw it over so that it swung back to him, and he tied a loop and pulled one end of the rope, fixing it tightly around the branch. Then he started swinging himself back and forth across the brook. He did his crow call several times and started swinging wildly, higher and higher; and then he began to laugh.

I watched him do this for about five minutes. He

landed back on the wall and tied a noose at his end of the rope. Was he going to hang himself? I waited, actually expecting the worst, but then he put one foot in the noose and started swinging back and forth again. Later he tried it with both feet in the loop. He seemed to be improvising little movements with his arms and legs, as if he were trying to construct a set of rope-swing maneuvers all his own. Had he forgotten me? I certainly didn't want to disturb him, he looked so happy and peaceful by himself.

It was as good a time as any for me to slide to the far edge of the roof and climb back down the drainpipe of Neil's garage. I managed to sneak back up the chimney and into my room. In bed again, I kept wondering if Eddie, eventually realizing that I wasn't coming, would go away anyhow. The next day I stayed in my own backyard throughout the morning, unable to think of anything to do. At such times it was my habit to wander over to Eddie's house, but this day was different. If I were to go over and discover that he had really gone, I would be sorry, tragically so, that I hadn't gone with him. Yet if he were home, what shame I would feel! What could I say to him?

I almost decided not to go over to Eddie's house, but my curiosity became too great. I walked into his backyard and found no one there except his mother and younger sister, Eileen. She was helping her mother unload some groceries from the car.

"Hi, Mrs. Reilly. Ed around?"

"I don't know, David. Haven't seen him."

She didn't know? Mrs. Reilly, a heavyset woman, had seven children, Eddie being the second youngest; and she never could keep track of them all. My God, I thought, Eddie might be in some freight car by now, halfway across the country, and still he hasn't even been missed!

Following my usual custom, I went down the steps to the Reillys' cellar. Walking past the washroom, which was piled with laundry, all I could see was his older brother's pool table and, along the far wall, Eddie's model-train layout (he had the most intricate layout of any kid I knew; he was able to run *four trains at once)*. The only light on was a naked bulb attached to a wire hanging down from the ceiling.

Suddenly one of the trains started moving. It ran down one of the tracks and around a corner. Then it went under a bridge, through a tunnel, and up an incline, where it took another corner. I watched it go around again and then called, "Eddie?"

The train stopped, as if it had a personality apart from its human controller. In the silence I called him again. Eddie's head popped up in the "engineer's circle" in the middle of the table.

"Ed? Hi. It's me, Dave."

"Hi," he grunted, without looking up.

As he started to tighten some tracks with a screwdriver, I tried to figure out if his face was more solemn than usual. I wondered how badly I had hurt his feelings, or disappointed him.

"Eddie, I'm sorry I didn't show up last night. I really am, Ed. My parents—they caught me trying to sneak out of the house. Honest, Ed. They really did. I was all set to go, to meet you at the bridge, but ..."

If Eddie was solemn, it was over his train layout, not over my failure to meet him the night before. I stood there in the cellar, watching as he intently worked on the model trains, and I began to realize that "going away" had meant much more to me than it had to him.

He ducked under the train table and grabbed a pool

stick. I watched him knock the cue ball around for a while. "No hard feelings, Ed?"

"What about?" he said, leaning against the billiard table and grinding the tip of his stick into the tiny square of blue chalk. He grinned slyly at me and said, almost in a whisper, "We could've been gone." I nodded my head. After a long silence he added, "And someday I *will* go, too."

I knew it was so; he *would* go away one day. And what a fool I had been to think that Eddie was depending on me, when it was just the other way around. All that summer, and for several years during our previous childhood, I had depended upon Eddie to make my world come alive and to transform my dull existence into something exciting. Eddie was the one kid who *least* needed to run away and yet, ironically or perhaps as a consequence, only he was truly free to leave.

"I'm gonna set up my trains outside," he said.

"Outside?"

"Yeah. Gonna get some plywood boards and set 'em up around the house with tracks on 'em. And then get a wire extension and put the transformer up in the tree fort. We can run the train from up there, and watch it go around the whole house."

Ordinarily I would have joined him eagerly, but I was too keenly aware of my dependence upon him. Something had happened to our friendship that made it impossible, now, for me to follow him.

"No," I said, "I gotta go."

"What for?"

"Oh, I got a million things to do."

Actually I had nothing at all to do, but I left him and went back to my house. I figured that if I couldn't create something interesting out of my own private world, I'd never be strong enough, like Eddie, to go away.

As soon as I got home, my parents asked me if I'd like to go to the Club for a swim. Unable to find a reason to stay home, I went with them. Right then I should have realized that I'd never be as free as Eddie, that I'd always be dependent on *something* to keep busy. But it's not that easy, it's not the happiest thing in the world, to admit that you don't have much going for you inside yourself.

2

Learning

Kids follow their parents' thinking for a long time, when they're growing up, and we were no exception. For example, I think there was a time when every kid on Valley Stream Road hated Stevenson and wore "I Like Ike" buttons, simply because our parents were Republicans. So were most people in Bushmont. Aside from the question of whether Eisenhower was a good president or not, it's a sad commentary to remember how viciously and stupidly we were taught to malign Stevenson. Kids at school used to sing, "Whistle while you work, Stevenson's a jerk," and they used to say, "Stevenson stinks," every time the subject was brought up. No one knew *why* he was such a bad fellow, but everyone was pretty sure about it, even emotional. You could see these really small kids putting down Stevenson. The veins in their heads stuck out, they got so worked up about it. And of course we all learned to believe that FDR had been a monster, again for reasons unknown.

The same can be said for religion. Eddie and Neil and Joyce and Ken and I were Catholics. We were taught that Protestants were misguided Catholics who had dropped out of the truth bag, and that Jews were the most selfish, obscene, and despicable people on earth. They were a threat to our community's character and to the morals of its fine citizens. The Jews were also supposed to be stupid, because they had rejected Christ even though He had been right in their midst. I'm sure my own parents would have rejected Him if He had come into *their* midst.

Anyway, there was one Jew on Valley Stream Road, named Mr. Greene. He didn't have any children, but we used to talk with him when he was outside clipping his hedge. I liked him a lot because he'd yell at us and then smile and call us over.

"Hey, you kids!" he'd yell. "Don't go on that grass or I'll eat you alive!" See, he knew what our parents said about him. Then he'd smile and say, "How tall do you think the tallest person on earth is?"

He'd tell us the craziest kind of information, most of which, I found out later, had come from "Ripley's Believe It Or Not." He made a big impression on me because he seemed to know about such whacky things. Like about the Chinese, how if you put them four abreast and march them through a gate, they'd never stop coming because of all the people in the rear of the parade who were being born, and so on. Things like that.

I had a real fondness for Mr. Greene, but my parents never bothered with him because he was Jewish. They were missing something by avoiding him. I knew that, even as a young kid. Mr. Greene was more intelligent and witty than most of the grown-ups in the neighborhood, including my own parents. He was the only adult who used four-letter words when he spoke to us kids, and that alone gave me a warm feeling toward him. And we could ask him all kinds of questions, about anything at all—mostly Eddie did the asking—and he'd give us a straight answer. My mother would say, "Where did you get *that* piece of information?" But I never ratted on Mr. Greene. He filled us in on things that my parents never would have discussed with me, and maybe things they didn't even discuss among themselves.

Mr. Greene's wife died when we were growing up,

and I remember how we all watched his house as if we were looking at Death Itself. My mother said, "Well, you know the Jews. He'll be married again within a year."

"Why do you say that, Mom?"

"Because," my father injected, "Jews do not share the concept of Christian love."

"And therefore," my mother added, "they cannot hold the Sacrament of Marriage in very high esteem."

My parents really had a low opinion of Jews, especially when it came to moral behavior. According to my folks, we Catholics had a monopoly on just about everything regarding the human spirit. I guess you could say that I was taught to love myself, or at least to believe that God was more on my side than on, say, Mr. Greene's.

He never did remarry, by the way. Now that I think of it, there would have been nothing wrong if he had. My folks would have shaken their fingers, though.

Which brings me to a sad little incident. A few months after Mr. Greene's wife died, Eddie and I gathered up a pile of dog shit in a paper bag, and we put it just outside Mr. Greene's front door. Then we lit a match to it, with some newspapers for a better flame. We watched from a distance, behind a bush, as Mr. Greene came outside and discovered the burning dog crap. Eddie and I were laughing like crazy. A few days later, we saw him clipping his hedge and he was his old self. He started telling us about how harmful cigarettes were. He used a handkerchief to show us the brown stains made by the nicotine in the smoke. He never even mentioned the dog crap we had burned on his doorstep.

A bit later, Eddie came over to my house and said he wanted to speak to me, alone, in my room. When we got up there he sat down on my bed and held his face in his hands.

"Why did we do it?" he asked.

"Do what?"

"What we did to Mr. Greene. Why?"

I noticed he was fighting back tears. He looked the way he had when the sunfish had died. Seeing him so emotional made me nervous, so I paced back and forth and agreed out loud that yes, we had done a terrible thing. We discussed it from beginning to end, but we couldn't remember *why* we had singled out Mr. Greene. He was one of our favorite grown-ups in the whole neighborhood! There were dozens of adults that we didn't like at all! Being sad and sorry about it was bad enough, but the worst part was that we didn't know why we had done it.

Eventually, we decided to go see Mr. Greene and apologize to him. We went up and rang his bell, and he was really surprised and glad to see us. He invited us inside and made us some ice cream sodas, and he showed us his book library. Eddie and I kept looking at each other, wondering which one of us was going to tell Mr. Greene about the dog shit. At last Eddie said, "Mr. Greene, we've got something to tell you." "Out with it, Eddie my boy."

"Well ..."

Eddie was having trouble choosing the right words, so I said, "Did you happen to find something burning in front of your house recently?"

"Mmmmm," said Mr. Greene. "Let me think. Oh, yes. I think I remember something along those lines."

"Well," Eddie joined in, "we did it."

"That's right," I said. "And we want to tell you that we're sorry."

Mr. Greene looked at us a moment and then wrinkled his nose. He said, "Whatever it was that you burned, it sure stunk like hell."

Eddie burst out laughing and so did I. As the tension left us we started roaring, and even Mr. Greene was chuckling. I thought Eddie and I would never be able to stop laughing. For about five minutes we had a real release.

Then we apologized again, and I noticed something come over Mr. Greene's face. I suddenly remembered that he was Jewish, the only Jew in our neighborhood, and I kind of knew why we had done it. I became frightened of something in myself, and I think Eddie did too. I felt awfully sorry for Mr. Greene right then. I wanted to touch him or something. He was smiling, but I could sense a deep pain inside him.

"I'm really sorry," I said again, but at the same time I was recalling my mother's cynical statement that Mr. Greene's original name was probably Greenburg. And I began to get angry at my parents, because I also blamed *them* for what I had done to Mr. Greene. I mean, you can't just do something cruel to a person and not have any reason at all for doing it.

After that, I noticed that Eddie was spending less time in his backyard. After school I'd rush over there, but nobody knew where he was. Neil and I spent a lot of time at the Reillys' basketball court (at the end of the driveway), but I'd always be wondering where Eddie could be. Around dinner time he'd show up and hardly say a word to us. He had a strange look on his face, as if he had just been through some kind of deeply moving experience. "Where've you been?" I asked him once.

"Just messing around," he replied.

One day after school I decided to follow him from a distance. He changed his clothes at home and then set out on foot through some backyards, stopping along the way to notice little things such as strange flowers or anything at all that was interesting to him, which seemed like just about everything. After about twenty minutes of roaming around, I realized he   was heading into Mr. Greene's backyard. I crouched behind some bushes and watched as he climbed the back steps and rang the doorbell. Mr. Greene answered, and Eddie went inside. I stayed around for a while, hoping to see them through a window, but it was no use. I went over to the Reillys' backyard and a few hours later, Eddie returned from whatever he had been doing with Mr. Greene. All kinds of things had been going through my mind — Mr. Greene was an atheist-homosexual who was molesting the mind and body of my friend!

When I was alone with Eddie one day, I told him that I knew about his secret meetings with Mr. Greene, and would he mind explaining to me what it was all about.

"History," he said with a shrug. "He tells me stories."

"What about?"

"Mostly about Jews and stuff. Things they don't tell you in school. You wouldn't believe some of it, David. You really wouldn't."

"What kind of things?"

"Oh, there's too much to tell," said my friend, who always had enjoyed listening more than talking, anyway.

Later on I noticed that every third weekend or so, Eddie went on special outings with Mr. Greene. He'd hop in Mr. Greene's car and they'd take off for most of a Saturday, or sometimes just for an hour or two.

"Where've you been going?" I finally asked him.

"Places."

"What places, Ed?"

"Well, last Saturday we went upstate and saw an insane asylum. One with bars on the windows and all."

"Really?"

"Yep. Went inside and saw some of the people and all."

"What was it like, Ed?"

He gave me a brief description of the insane asylum, but not enough details for me to form a real picture of it in my mind.

"Where else have you gone?" I asked.

"Oh, one time we went down to the Bowery, in New York. And Chinatown, the same day. We also went down to the Flats and walked around one time. Looked at all the colored people."

"What for? I mean, why?"

"Because," he said, smiling at me with a little gleam in his eyes, "it's almost like being gone."

I looked at my friend for a long moment, wondering how it could be possible that he seemed, already, so much older than me. How could we grow up on the same street and start becoming so different? I wished that I could join him in his meetings and outings with Mr. Greene, but I didn't dare ask. I suppose I still felt bad about not having met him at the bridge.

And besides, I told myself in a burst of new confidence, I wasn't so sure that I wanted to go to such places and listen to Jewish history, anyway. So the hell with it, I thought with pleasure.

I forgot to mention that one direct result of being Catholic was that the Valley Stream Stinkers didn't go to the public grade schools. To our parents, it was a sin for Catholics to send their kids to a public school if they could do otherwise. As for college, we began to hear about the evils of *that* scene from the third grade on. I don't know how many times I heard that places like Harvard or Columbia University were filled with Jews and atheists (synonymous terms for my parents) waiting to blacken my soul and drain me of spiritual grace. It was to be Catholic college for us, or nothing.

Up through the eighth grade, we took the bus back

and forth across Bushmont, to and from Holy Family School. In later years I thought how ironical that was, because my parents became firm opponents of busing for school integration in the elementary grades.

One time in grade school our whole class was going to go to Mass at nine o'clock to receive Holy Communion. I had forgotten about it and had eaten breakfast. This was a fault, because you weren't supposed to eat any food up to three hours before going to Communion. The nun told us to line up in the hall before going into the church. I said to her, "Sister, I can't receive this morning."

"Why not, David?"

"I just can't."

"Have you been to Confession?"

"Yes, Sister, but—"

"Then you *can* receive."

"No, Sister, I can't."

"YOU CAN. YOU WILL."

With that, we went into church and sat in the front pews for Mass. When it came time for Communion, the nun clapped her hands together like a military commander. I stood up with the rest of the class and went to the Communion rail. If I took the Communion, I would be damned to hell for all eternity—unless I could make it to the Confessional booth before I died, of course—since I had eaten breakfast. If I *didn't* take the bread, however, the nun would fly into a rage and punish me. A decision like this, under such pressure, was worse than anything I could think of. The priest was coming along the rail, mumbling his Latin and placing the Body of our Lord on everybody's tongue. I stuck out my tongue and took the wafer, but in a quick motion, pretending to cough, I spit the wafer into my hands. I put it into the pocket of my dark-green Holy Family jacket and went back to the pew.

After Mass we returned to our room, hungry and thinking only of lunch, and I raised my hand.

"What is it now, David?"

"Sister, what would happen if someone took Communion, but didn't swallow it?"

"David, that's not possible."

"What if they did, though?"

"Are you trying to be funny?"

"No, Sister. What if someone pretended to receive Communion, but actually didn't?"

"I still don't follow you, David. *Explain yourself quickly.*"

"What would happen if, say, someone flushed their Holy Communion down the toilet?"

Now, anyone who hasn't seen a nun lose her temper would not fully appreciate the scene that followed. How is it that nuns, of all the human beings I can think of, aside from priests and Christian Brothers, have such short tempers? When I was going to school, they were always just a step away from pulling a boy along by his ear or hair and even slapping him in the face. Their hands shot out like the tongues of poisonous snakes. I can still hear the ringing in the hallway from a slap across the cheek that one nun gave to a boy.

This time, the nun rustled down the aisle between the desks and landed a blow on my head that I have never forgotten. She didn't say a word, just administered her blows until I moved my head, and her hand came crashing down against the edge of my desk. I knew she hurt her hand, because she began hitting me all over again, even harder. Eddie Reilly went into convulsions, and the nun sent him out to the hall to be dealt with later. This exchange between her and Eddie only made *me* laugh, which nearly drove the nun crazy.

By the way, nuns never hit girls, not that I recall. This could have been because they were partial to them, but it was probably also because girls, especially Joyce Clarkson, were such brown noses in grade school. I must say that Joyce was a classic case, though. Outside the school she'd say things like, "That Sister Margaret can stick it up her ass," and other vivid remarks, while in the classroom you'd have thought she was Saint Bernadette.

Anyhow, the nun, after hitting me, went back to the front of the class and shouted, "I'll tell you, David! I'll tell you the truth! Our Lord's Body would *bleed*, and the water in the bowl would become red with His Blood! Does that answer your foolish question?"

"Yes, Sister."

Actually I was planning to eat the wafer as soon as it was three hours past the time I had eaten breakfast. But the nun's retort had introduced a most fascinating possibility. Imagine making Christ bleed in the toilet bowl! A miracle in the Boys' Room!

At lunch time I went to the lavatory and flipped Our Lord into the toilet. I watched Him float a moment and then settle to the bottom. I flushed Him down. When nothing happened, I thought about cutting my finger, dripping the blood, and inviting the nun inside for a real eye-widening experience. I would take my place among guys like Lazarus and St. Paul. Maybe they'd put a big sign in front of the school—St. David of Latrine!—with a statue of me bending over a big bronze toilet bowl.

It sounds like a ridiculous episode, but in fact it was serious business. The nun had lied to me, which of course I had suspected, but it raised a matter of even more importance than casual hypocrisy. See, what she had said, about Our Lord bleeding and so on, was the natural, logical answer to my question. And that was frightening. She really believed that the wafer was the Body of Jesus Christ. I did, too! If you don't believe that, then you've got to throw out the entire significance, the reality, of the Mass.

So what about this "transubstantiation" thing we were being taught? What about my immortal soul? Was everything not real but symbolic? The Catholic religion teaches you right away that you've got an eternal soul that'll go up to heaven or down to hell when you die. Those nuns and priests, they scared the holy shit out of us Catholic kids. We all walked around with the idea that we had souls inside us that looked like big aspirin tablets. The nun used to draw them on the blackboard! If you committed a sin, the aspirin tablet got a black blotch on it. The nun drew that in, too. The more you sinned, the blacker it got. The nun almost ran out of chalk trying to demonstrate how this God-inspired method of slow spiritual death worked. And what's more, she seemed to *enjoy* the way God could be such a torture freak. If you had a *mortal-sin* blotch on there, forget it. You would have gone straight down into the fire if you died. Draw those flames, Sister! It takes years, sometimes a whole life, occasionally longer, to shake off a crazy idea like that.

3

Schooling

When I was around fifteen, the soul problem got really bad. Every Saturday we ran into the church for Confession so the priest would make our aspirin tablets all white again. You come out feeling like you've just taken a hot bath with plenty of soap. An hour later, you start French-kissing a girl and as soon as her tongue hits yours all you can think of is BLACK MARK! I GOT A BLACK MARK! After the first new black blotch is on there, though, you start loosening up. After all, what's a few more? What's a few more flames when you're already down there burning?

But next week, on Saturday, you start getting ready to go back to Confession all over again. That was the day the priest was in there in his booth in the church. So you go in there and kneel in the dark, with your face against the gauze, and you say, "Bless me, Father, for I have sinned. It's been exactly one week since my last Confession. Since then I've French-kissed a girl seventy-three times."

"Anything else, son?"

"Well, I masturbated eleven times."

"Anything else, my boy?"

"I put my hand on a girl's chest eight and a half times."

"Eight and a *half*?"

"Yes, Father. I was halfway there when her mother walked in."

"Was this the same girl that you kissed seventy-three times in a mortally sinful way?"

"No, Father. There were two separate girls."

"I see. Two separate souls that you have helped to blacken."

"Yes, Father."

"Uh hunh. And the masturbation, is this something you do in the same circumstances each time?"

"No, Father."

"How many kinds of circumstances?"

"All kinds, Father. A lot of times in bed, if that's any help."

"I see, in bed. Perhaps you should go to bed from now on only when you're very tired, and ready to fall asleep. And get out of bed as soon as you wake up in the morning. Take a cold shower. Don't give yourself a chance."

"I'll try that, Father," I lied, thereby committing a sin during the very act of confessing my sins. What **I** didn't want to tell him was that I also masturbated, while fully clothed, when lying on top of girls. I didn't know quite how to describe that to him.

"Is there anything else, young man?"

"I don't think so, Father, unless you want to include the unclean thoughts that I had when I did the other stuff."

"Hmmmm."

"So, that wraps it up, Father."

"Weren't you in here last week, son?"

"Uh, yes, Father. I was."

"With the same confession?"

"Just about, I guess. Same sins, different numbers."

"Do you plan to come in here next week with the same list of sins?"

"No, I don't *plan* to, Father. But don't be surprised if **I** do."

"Are you making a True Confession? Do you resolve to try and avoid these sins? Perhaps you had better promise not to see those two girls again."

"I'll try my best, Father."

At this point the priest usually has raised his voice to a sufficiently high level so that the person in the other side of the booth can probably hear you.

"For your penance say six *Our Fathers* and six *Hail Marys*, and be a good boy."

"Thank you, Father."

And so on, all through the seasons and the years, until one day you start feeling so hypocritical that you have to make **a** choice between the black marks and the clean-white aspirin tablet. Besides, this priest is getting a little exasperated. And you're embarrassed. The damn priest probably knows who you are! He sees you walking outside and you say, "Hello, Father," and he probably recognizes your voice! He's thinking, "I'll bet that kid masturbated today. It doesn't look like he's taken a shower." Or he sees you with a girl and thinks that she's either the one you've been fondling or French-kissing or dry-humping, although the girl might only be your cousin or even your mother.

One time, in the Confessional booth, the younger priest in our parish called me by my *name*. He said, "Is that all, *David?*" I nearly threw up on the spot.

So you've either got to stop committing sins or stop going to Confession. Stop French-kissing? Stop jerking off? Stop feeling tit? Stop *thinking?*

No, better to stop going to Confession. And if you cross that bridge, then you can't go to Communion anymore, because your soul is so black. I'll never forget being in mortal sin, sitting in church in one of the rear pews, watching all the good folks going up to the rail and sticking out their pious tongues for the little round pieces of bread. My mother would poke me and whisper, "Aren't you going to receive, David?"

"No," I'd whisper back.

"Why not?"

"I ate a piece of coffee cake this morning, by mistake," I'd lie.

It's crazy, but when you go to Mass, the Big Moment is when it comes time for Communion. Maybe 20 percent of the congregation goes up to the rail for it (probably less, these days). You have to figure that those who remain seated are either in sin or undergoing digestion, or both. Probably most of the people who don't go to Communion are in mortal sin, it's impossible to tell. I used to watch their faces. Most of them, like me, would try to act unconcerned. Some sinners would pretend to be reading their Missals while everyone went to Communion. See, there's no reason at all to pray if you're in mortal sin. It doesn't do you a damn bit of good until you get *out* of mortal sin. So pretending to read your Missal was a terrific cover-up.

But if you don't go to Communion, there are only two reasons why. Either you've eaten food or you're in sin. Or both. What really upset me was when my mother *knew* that I hadn't eaten any breakfast or coffee cake or anything. Then, when I didn't go up to the rail, she *had* to figure that her son was all fouled-up in his soul. Very embarrassing, when your own mother knows you're in sin. Every aspect of it was embarrassing.

What I hated even more was to sit there and watch all the little girls, many of whom I had French-kissed or fondled or dry-humped during the preceding week. Sometimes a girl would go to Confession on Saturday afternoon, get fondled by me that night, and therefore be unable to receive Communion the next morning. I lost a lot of Saturday-night dates after a while. I was a total bastard. One time I saw a girl that I had fondled the night before. She was sitting across the aisle from me in church, and when it came time for Communion, naturally she didn't go. Neither did I, of course. I caught her attention and waved. Wow, did she blush. But those who had gone to Confession and who had *escaped* my clutches on Saturday night were right there in the church, happily parading up to Communion. Happily isn't the word. They went up to that rail like *saints.* They'd look at me out of the corners of their eyes, noticing that I wasn't receiving. I felt terrible, sitting there with my ugly black soul. My aspirin tablet was so blotched up that there wasn't any *room* for any more sins.

I'd sit there watching the faces of these little Madonnas as they marched back from the Communion rail. They'd have their hands folded, heads down, eyes closed, and some even wore veils. They looked like floating geese under hypnosis. I don't know how they knew where they were going, or how in hell they managed to avoid bumping into the pews or other people or even into the walls.

And me, I hadn't been to Communion or Confession in weeks or months. I had chalked up over six hundred French kisses, at least a hundred fondles and as many masturbations, including a few innovative sins as well. Imagine going to Confession and giving *those* figures to a priest. I might as well have *murdered* someone, with all those black marks. I definitely had cancer of the aspirin tablet. I felt like a devil who was going to start putting black marks on the good little girls' souls in the very near future. They'd see me coming after church and I figured they were thinking, "Here comes a black mark!" A terrible burden on me, a big responsibility. Imagine if I gave one of them a black mark and she *died* before getting to

Confession on Saturday! With a blotch on her soul that I had given her!

Yet the amusing thing, the funny thing, was that *they* started the French-kissing bit, not me. I had never even known the *existence* of French-kissing until one night when a girl almost broke my teeth trying to get her tongue in there. Those damn hypocritical girls who posed as Virgin Marys every Sunday morning! Another girl, one of the more sublime of the floating geese, whom I called The Locomotive, had picked up the habit of grabbing my pants zipper every time we were alone. She would bring along a special packet of tissues in her purse specially for me whenever I took her out. We'd be sitting in her back porch listening to records and I'd see her opening her little maroon purse. Out would come the tissues and a secret code signal that she'd give me every time the make-David-come ritual was to begin. Without realizing she was doing it, she'd say in a half-whisper, "Choo choo." That's all: "Choo choo." Which is why I privately called her The Locomotive. She and I would be sitting under a tree somewhere and I'd hear, "Choo choo." Aha! The Locomotive had developed an amazingly reliable animal call, with me as the animal. She gave the signal, I had an instant erection. What I wondered was if she really confessed to the priest that she jerked me off. She went in that Confessional booth and was out in thirty seconds. I used to take her to Confession, but not go myself. One time she came out of the booth and I said, "Choo choo!" That really cracked her up.

And how come the girls never seemed to feel as hypocritical about all that as I did? I began to despise Catholic girls, possibly for that very reason. Seeing a girl walking like a saint back from the Communion rail, especially one who has whacked you off several times during the preceding week, is like listening to a crooked politician make a campaign speech. Somebody's kidding somebody.

4

Eddie's Spirit

Eddie Reilly never seemed to have these problems, even though he was raised as a Catholic like me and went to Holy Family School like I did. First of all, I figured, he never went out with girls at that age. It was his opinion that girls were a waste of time, and besides, I thought he was shy. But even if he had gone out with Catholic girls then, I don't think the religious nonsense would have bothered him. As in most everything else, Eddie just accepted the fact that he was born a Catholic and then dismissed it from his mind. He didn't fight against things. He hardly ever went to church, and even less often to Confession or Communion. Occasionally he'd go, but only when he felt like it. One time I asked him if it worried him that he was in mortal sin, and he replied, "Why am I in mortal sin?"

"Because you haven't been to Mass for three weeks, that's why."

"So what's that got to do with mortal sin?"

For Christ's sake, didn't he listen to the nun in class at *all?* "Listen, Reilly, it's a mortal sin if you don't go to Mass on Sunday. You know that as well as I do."

"Who says?"

"The *Church* says, idiot."

"Well, *I* say that it's *not* a mortal sin."

"If I killed you right now, Eddie, you'd go straight to hell."

Eddie broke up. He loved that one. Chuckling away in the high-decibel range, he said, "And what about *you,*

Dave? You'd be the *murderer*."

"I could still go to Confession," I said, laughing with him, "and confess it. Then I'd go to *heaven* if I died."

"First you'd go to *jail*," he said.

Eddie seemed to have his own religious standards and maybe even his own religion, I didn't know. If he didn't like the rules he just changed them for himself. Or more accurately, he disregarded them. Me, I eventually had to denounce the Church and God and everything, while Eddie, when pressed, would casually state that he "sort of" believed in God. While I was the one who denounced religion, I was still more attached to it than he was. The same in regard to Bushmont Village, which I often denounced bitterly for being such a dull and comfortable and hypocritical place. Eddie, like his secret tutor, Mr. Greene, never seriously got emotional about it, not the way I did. He was simply free of it. He really had his own world.

Although he felt that girls were a waste of time and effort, I don't mean to give the impression that he had no *interest* in them. He was as hung up over the sight of bouncing tits as the next guy, but he just hated to go through the ritual of asking a girl out, picking her up in a taxi, meeting her parents, spending money on her, and making stupid conversation. Despite all this, the girls went for him. Eddie was built very solidly and had extremely good features. The girls said he had great eyes. They called him "cute," which sent him into an absolute rage.

If they only knew! He undoubtedly *was* cute, but the girls might have felt a bit differently if they had known about his peephole operation at the Bushmont Beach and Yacht Club. Eddie discovered that with a nail or a drill you could make small peepholes in the side walls of the bathhouse lockers. From that discovery, he invented Operation Peephole.

Half of the lockers were "permanent" ones, meaning that they belonged to certain families for the season, and the other half were "transient" lockers, for anyone who wanted to use the bathhouse for just a few hours. The two types of locker rooms were spread all over the bathhouse, but next to each other. Eddie would get into a transient locker and drill a few discreet holes in each wall. Eventually every transient locker had peepholes on both walls, courtesy of Edward Reilly.

We'd sit out in front of the bathhouse and play cards or pretend to be waiting for somebody. When a girl came in, we'd say hello to her and then look at our Permanent Locker Chart, which Eddie had drawn up. If the girl's permanent locker was Number Twenty, for example, we'd go ask for the key to Transient Locker Number Twenty-Two, right next to it. We'd make sure the girl was in her locker first, and then we'd slip into ours. Once in a while we got there ahead of her, which was even better, or safer.

Eddie and I would crouch down and peek through our respective holes to watch the girl undress. Sometimes we'd get to view as many as five or six undressed girls, in one day. We must have seen Joyce Clarkson about twenty times. Over a whole summer, it added up to a lot of girls. It was great to see them afterward, all dressed up or in bathing suits, because you could imagine them from in the bathhouse.

Sometimes a girl would unwittingly drape a piece of clothing on a hook so that it blocked one of the peepholes. The guy who was looking through that hole would go crazy, and usually a struggle for the remaining clear hole followed, with the result that neither of us would see her. After several of these emergencies, Eddie began drilling what he called "auxiliary" holes.

Watching those girls was a fantastic experience, at the time, not only because we got to see them naked but because they did such unexpected things. One girl masturbated right in front of my wide-open eyeball. I had never even known that girls *did* that. Another girl, a blond, had black pubic hair, which led us to the conclusion that she used bleach for the hair on her head. Another naked girl put on a hat and danced in front of her mirror, wiggling her tits like a madwoman. Eddie started laughing with that contagious falsetto of his, and we both had to run out of the locker. I was sure she had heard us.

We not only watched girls, but men and women of all ages, from twelve to ninety. Eddie would make whispered comments like, "Cow! What a cow!" or, "Ugh!" A real lesson in the diversity of the human body. One time we watched the parents of one of our friends undress. That was really weird. What made it stranger was that they never looked at each other while they were naked. He faced one way, and she faced the other. When they backed up, their rear ends would touch, and the two of them would giggle.

On another occasion, a woman about fifty years old suddenly bent down and looked through my peephole. She and I were staring at each other, literally eyeball-to-eyeball. I jumped back and quickly placed the tip of my finger over the hole. Eddie and I held our breath, waiting for the woman to let out a shriek. Almost a minute went by, so I took my finger away and bent down again. Looking through the hole, I met once more with the woman's eyeball. I jumped back and put my fingertip over the hole for the second time. Suddenly a sharp object sank into my finger. *Yow!* The old gal had stuck a pin into me! Again we had to beat it out of the locker.

See, the peephole operation was mostly fun, not so much because of what we saw but because of the intrigue. There was always the chance of being caught in the act. Eddie scorned the Bushmont Beach and Yacht Club, but Operation Peephole gave him a way to transcend it, which was Eddie Reilly's normal way of adapting to places and situations that he didn't like.

By the end of the first and only full summer of Operation Peephole activity, I had left the Confessional booth far behind. Strange, then, that one night my father came into my bedroom, closed the door behind him, and sat down on the edge of the bed to "discuss whatever may be on our minds." I had no idea what was on *his* mind, but I nodded solemnly. Anyhow, it turned out to be the classic father-son "serious" discussion which was, as must usually be the case, at least three years too late to matter. The old man started hemming and hawing about all kinds of mysterious things, and I almost felt like saying, "Bless me, Father, for I have sinned." It was really ridiculous.

My father very seriously explained to me that if a male seed gets to a female egg, there might be some big trouble up ahead. I assured him that I knew about that, but he repeated it all over again. Then we hovered around the matter of whacking off, and again I offer an absolutely unoriginal anecdote.

"David," he said, "do you ever feel like, uh, rubbing yourself?"

"Rubbing myself, Dad?"

"Yes. You know. Rubbing yourself."

"Where?"

"Down there."

"Down where?"

"Between your legs."

I looked at my father for a moment, and then turned my head, pretending to give the matter some thought. I said, "Well, sometimes I get an itch, you know?" I was really being terrible to my poor old man. I shouldn't have acted that way, but I couldn't have just come out and said, "Yes! Yes, Dad! I do! I *always* feel like rubbing myself down there!" That would have been the truer, but dumber, way to reply.

"I don't mean an itch," he said. "I mean something perfectly natural, that you don't have to be ashamed of."

I didn't? Was my father going to tell me that it was *all right* to masturbate? Was it possible?

"It's perfectly natural, that feeling," he went on, sounding like he was ready to announce that I was pregnant, "but I think you should know, if you already don't, that it would be better if you *don't* rub yourself down there."

"Okay, Dad. I'll remember that. Thanks a lot."

"Because if you do, the Church regards it as a mortal sin."

Ah! I suddenly had an urge to disagree with him: "How can it be a mortal sin if it's perfectly natural?"

The old man's face turned red for some reason, but he quickly replied, "Because sex is for a man and a woman, for the two of them together, in marriage, so they can have children. That's why."

I nodded my head slowly.

Then he said, "I told you that the *feeling*, or the *urge*, is natural, but it requires a female, in marriage." He paused a moment and then came out with another classic announcement. "If you do it alone," he said, "it can cause brain damage."

I'm not kidding, he said it. I know it's almost material for a nightclub act, or at best something that people might have believed at some distant time, and I'm sure *he* didn't believe it, but he really said it.

"Brain damage, Dad?"

"That's right, son. It very possibly could do something to your mind. The point I'm making is that you shouldn't do it. I advise you, as your father, to play it safe. Anything unnatural is potentially harmful."

"I thought you said it was natural."

"I said the *feeling* is natural."

"Oh."

After he left and shut off the lights, I turned over in bed and masturbated. With gusto. All I had to do was lie on my stomach and push myself back and forth a few times. But I almost believed my father, that was the terrible thing. I thought about what he had said and came to the conclusion that if masturbation causes brain damage, then intercourse must be some magical thing whereby the nerve endings that connect up to your brain are deactivated.

For a while I actually became concerned about the whole thing. Four or five days after my father's talk, an event which he probably had been planning for a decade, I began walking around thinking that maybe I was going insane. Brain damage! Wow, if that were true, my father had been much too late in coming forth with the warning. I should have been far gone already. Paradoxically, I doubled my whacking-off man-hours during this time of anxiety. Like the ordeal with the black marks, if I was already half-insane, why not go all the way?

The trouble with me was that I always took things too seriously. Or maybe I took the *wrong* things seriously. I believed what people told me and I pushed things to their logical conclusions. I was an extremist, I decided, and that was either very good or very bad. I'd always discover this aspect of myself when I was airing my thoughts with Eddie Reilly. I went to him and said, "Hey, Ed, did you know that whacking off can give you brain damage?"

See, I was serious, but he started howling and rolling over and over on the grass lawn in front of his house. That solved the question right then and there. But for at least six months, Eddie kept reminding me of it and laughing all over again.

Right in the middle of a crowd he'd whisper, "Brain damage," and curl up in hysterics. Eddie Reilly, has anyone in the world ever laughed as much as you did?

Things just didn't affect him the way they did me. I became angry in the extreme over the things I had been led to believe — like that Christ would bleed in the toilet, or that I had an aspirin tablet with black marks, or that Jews would litter the beach, or that war was something to romanticize, or that whacking off would cause brain damage, or that Stevenson stank, or that Protestants were misguided fools, and so on down the list. Add them up and if you were really gullible and impressionable like I was, you'd have turned out a religious fanatic or an atheist, a warmonger or an ultra-pacifist, an extreme left- or right-winger, a racist, and a sexual wreck.

Eddie was one of the few people who could make me look at myself with a sense of humor. Then why, I wondered, did he seem so sad lately? Why, if he was able to laugh so wildly that his brown eyes seemed to sparkle, was he so withdrawn, so pensive, so moody? And why, most of all, did I find myself imitating his moodiness every once in a while? Was it because I *admired* the way he could sit in the corner of a room all night without saying anything? He seemed so self-contained, as if there were an invisible shell around him.

One night, at a party, I walked up to him and said, "What's the matter, Eddie boy?"

"Nothing."

"What are you thinking about so hard?"

"Concentration camps."

Oh, did I have a laugh over *that* one. I slapped him on the knee, saying something about the fact that he had a weird sense of humor, and went back to the party. Only later on did it occur to me that he might have been serious.

He had stopped seeing Mr. Greene so frequently, but now I noticed that he was branching out, so to speak. He'd come over to my house and start talking with Ella, our colored cleaning lady; and sometimes he'd walk with her into the Village, where she caught a bus for the Flats in downtown Brookdale.

"You moved away from Birmingham after three years," I once heard him saying to her, "but where were you living *before* that time?"

Somehow I was embarrassed that he was talking so intimately with my parents' black maid. Ella would laugh at his questions and try to brush them off, but Eddie persisted until she gave him a straight answer. And after that, he'd get her to fill in more information, pursuing it down to the tiniest detail.

But he was branching out to several people, not only Ella. It seemed that my little friend had an insatiable curiosity. He talked (listened, rather) for hours to some Italian gardeners who worked at his house, and sometimes he'd walk along with the postman, pumping him with questions.

Also, there was this guy with one arm in our neighborhood, named Pete, who was probably near thirty years old. His arm had been sliced off about five inches from the shoulder, and I think he had become a little retarded. I learned from Eddie that Pete had been in a car accident at an early age. I was with Eddie one time when he asked Pete all about his arm — how it felt, what he could or couldn't do with only one hand, and then my friend asked if he could *touch* the remainder of Pete's missing arm. Pete seemed a bit suspicious, yet pleased; and he let Eddie put his hand up the empty shirtsleeve. Touching the arm stub, Eddie smiled a little at Pete, who suddenly lost his look of suspicion and distrust.

Right in front of my eyes, the two of them had become lasting friends.

5

God and the Devil

To me, growing up in Bushmont was an isolation from the outside world, but being sent to Catholic school served to doubly remove us from reality. All the way up to the eighth grade, the girls and boys were required to wear uniforms to school. We had to line up in the asphalt schoolyard behind the church while the nuns, their robes and beads fluttering in the wind, clapped their palms together like sergeants in boot camp. God was sternly injected into every possible subject, including arithmetic. We learned the damn multiplication table in terms such as "five angels times six angels equals thirty angels." The nun told us that each kid had a special angel. The angel followed you around wherever you went, and if you sinned, you'd hurt the winged creature's feelings. Ken Starro went around actually *talking* to his special angel. I'm surprised that Holy Family School didn't turn out more psycho cases than it did.

After eighth grade, Eddie and Ken and I were enrolled in Blessed Mother Prep School, about four miles away from our homes, while Joyce went to St. Mary's Academy and Neil went on to Brookdale High School. We purchased Blessed Mother windbreakers and Blessed Mother book bags, and caught the Blessed Mother bus every morning and afternoon. And we rooted for the Blessed Mother football team. I remember looking up at the scoreboard one time and seeing BLESSED MOTHER VS. SAINT JOSEPH. It was sort of like an athletic fantasy, or religious drama, with the teams symbolizing the two sides of a marital spat between Jesus Christ's parents. "Blessed Mother Trounces St. Joseph," ran one headline in the local sports page.

I think that Blessed Mother Prep School was a step closer to an Orwellian nightmare. Grade school had cut us off from kids of other religions and backgrounds, and had whittled down our minds to as narrow a vision as might seem tolerable, but Blessed Mother really *warped* us. First of all, we were cut off from girls. That might have been fine for Eddie, but I had sex on my mind all the time. I couldn't wait for three o'clock, to get out of school and rush to meet one of the girls from Trinity School or St. Mary's. It got so that I was living in two worlds, with almost a split personality. The Christian Brothers were always drilling us on the evils of sex, and I would wallow in guilt and apprehension. Hellfire and damnation! But after school, I'd rush off to be gratified by a current girlfriend.

"A woman's body is a temple!" shouted Brother McKay, who was our four-foot-tall teacher known as The Mouse. He was so little that he sometimes had to stand on his desk to deliver a sermon. He never asked us to *think,* just to *listen.* His little mouse-head stuck up from his black robes, and he strode around like Napoleon in tiny black pointed shoes with high heels. His face would get purple, actually purple, when he lectured on sex, which was several times a day. We could be studying *Romeo and Juliet* and he'd find a way to make it sound like Shakespeare had written a sequel to the Catechism.

"Yes, every woman is a temple! You should look at a female body and regard it as Christ's Own Church!" I tried. I really tried. On other occasions he'd use a different analogy. "Every time you're with a girl, I want you to repeat to yourself over and over: 'This is the Virgin Mary. This is the Virgin Mary.'" Again I tried. A girl would be lying on top of me, dry-humping like crazy, and I'd repeat to myself, "This is the Virgin Mary. This is the Virgin Mary."

Why did I take all this so seriously? Very few of the other guys did. They didn't seem to. Me, I almost *enjoyed* listening to The Mouse tell me how dirty and low and full of sin I was. I sweated all over and my heart pounded as he poured his invective upon us. "Carriers of the Devil!" Man, I just *shook* with fear. Then I'd glance over at Eddie Reilly, who'd be moving his eyebrows up and down, giggling!

It was grotesque. The predominant emotions in that school were hatred and fear, with a backlash of immature rebellion. Mainly what bothered me was that we didn't learn to *think* about anything, to become curious and open-minded. All we got were threats and questions to memorize. And every time I saw a Brother coming, I flinched a little in expectation of getting hit or yelled at. The usual method of punishment was a wide rubber strap, used on the open palms. All I remember is the punishment, not the offenses. You had to open your hands and hold them, palms up, in front of the Christian Brother. Then he'd whack you on each hand until the palms were stinging. They seemed to like the crackling sound of the strap against your skin. It was almost an erotic thing, if that makes any sense.

The irony about all this is that the discipline produced just the opposite effect from the one intended. The parents of most Catholic kids were really in love with the discipline aspect. They were more concerned with that than with education, if you ask me.

They *equated* it with education. But the truth is that the Catholic schools produced the worst pack of immature jerks imaginable.

For example, because we were cut off from girls and had it drummed into us that just about all forms of social intercourse were either Potentially or Actually sinful, a large percentage of the guys became sex maniacs. By the time they got halfway through Blessed Mother, they thought of girls as objects, nothing more. Objects either to stay away from or to climb all over. How in the world were we supposed to think of girls as human beings? As temples, maybe, or even as Virgin Marys, but not as people. As *whores*, but not as friends.

Also, by telling us that we were a pack of animals, the Brothers nearly turned us into just that. I'm not joking. The place where I heard the most obscenity and irreverence was Blessed Mother Prep School. Guys went around the corridors of the school goosing each other and giving the Finger to the Brothers behind their backs. In English class, every time we'd read something even remotely having to do with women, the guys would go into hysterics. We had these religious-instruction books, and not one was without a cry of bewildered lust scribbled inside it. "Christ died for your cock." "The Immaculate Contraceptive." And so forth. I'd go to the movies with guys from Blessed Mother and they acted like maniacs during every kissing scene. One kid used to whack off right in the theatre as soon as Doris Day appeared. A piece of literature was looked upon as either dull or pornographic, regardless of its artistic or literary merit. The Brothers condemned just about every American novel written in the twentieth century because most of the authors didn't seem to believe in God. A priest could win over his entire audience of Blessed

Mother boys by opening his remarks with the most ridiculous off-color joke. Not even off-color, but *suggestive*. Everything was out of proportion, exaggerated and contorted. Our examinations consisted mainly of lists of questions, the answers to which we had already memorized. Have you ever seen someone try to fit his memorized answers to the wrong set of questions? One time a Brother gave us the wrong test, by mistake, and half the class filled it with the answers to the test they had memorized. I think even the Brother was embarrassed, because obviously he hadn't taught us to do anything except become parrots. A guy could score a perfect mark on a test without ever using his brain, without ever thinking for himself.

A handful of guys, including Kenny, became so religious that they, too, couldn't relate to anything more alive than a statue. They'd follow their favorite Brothers around like goddamn *apostles*. They all genuflected every time a statue fell inside their fields of vision, and poor Ken nodded every time someone said the word "Jesus" within his hearing. You were *supposed* to nod your head, in fact. But Kenny looked as if he was continually ducking for apples. We used to tease him by repeating Christ's name over and over so he'd have to keep nodding like an idiot. When he got angry, he sounded and sort of acted like a "fairy" and this drove the other guys wild. There was a rumor that Kenny and one of the Brothers were homosexuals, and that they were having a big affair. The whole thing was sick, one way or the other. Eventually the real religious guys either joined the Seminary or went nuts trying to adjust to the real world. I know for a fact that two of them had nervous breakdowns in college and that several others became vocal atheists. They were extremists like me, because they had been sucked in.

Would anyone believe that I suddenly decided that I wanted to be a priest? Impossible? "God worketh in strange ways," we were told. "His plan is not always apparent for an individual soul." Not always, in fact hardly ever. Either that or it's so damn apparent that God must be a pretty poor planner. Like a kid dying at one year old. Was that His plan? Way to go, God. Great plan.

But anyway, we were filled with stories about how St. Paul got knocked right off his horse and how St. Augustine was the biggest sinner around before becoming a Man of God. So there was all kinds of hope for me. I didn't get knocked off a horse, but I really did think that I should be a priest.

"Our goal in life," we were told, "is to become as much like Christ as possible. Being a bachelor is one vocation, but the least perfect one. The married state is fine, but becoming a priest is the highest calling one can receive. To be a priest, you have to be called by God. Many are called, but few are chosen. You have to be called *and* chosen by God."

I walked around hearing little voices in my head. Is that you, God? Are you calling me? But the voices, according to the teaching, could also be the Devil. Is that you, Devil?

"How do you know who's talking to you," I asked Brother McKay, "God or the Devil?"

"You'll know, David."

Thanks. Big help. But one day I had this wild dream about how The Bomb had been dropped, and I woke up hearing strange music and an announcer in my head saying, "David, be a priest! Be a priest!"

I told my mother and my father, "I've had a calling. A real calling!"

"A what?" said my father.

"I had a dream about the bomb."

"What bomb?"

"*The* bomb."

"So?"

"So then I had a calling."

"What the hell is a calling, goddamn it?"

"A calling from God."

"From who?"

"Whom," said my mother.

"From God. He wants me to be a priest."

"Now, David," said my father, becoming concerned, "how in hell do you know that God wants you to become a priest?"

"Stop swearing," my mother warned him.

"Because I got a calling, Dad. Can't you understand that?"

"No, I can't. How did He get in touch with you? By telegram?"

"In my head, Dad. In my heart. In my soul."

My mother's eyes filled up with tears and she made the Sign of the Cross. My father paced about for a moment and then shouted, "Well, tell Him to get in touch with me, will you? I'd like to talk it over with Him. I'd like to know if I should keep putting away money to send you to college."

"My son!" shouted my mother. "A priest!"

I left while the two of them argued over my calling. I was worried about dying, in the first place. That dream about The Bomb had clinched it; I should become a priest. After all, the whole thing about Christ is a clear choice. Either you believe in life-after-death, or you don't. All the theology in the world can't help you if you don't want to believe. I did want to believe, because I was afraid of dying, especially of going to hell. As the nuns had said in a moment of desperation (quoting Pascal, I think), it does no harm to believe in eternity and it may do us a lot of good (oh, yeah?).

Also, I really did want to become like Christ. Wouldn't it be great to walk around Bushmont like Jesus had done in His hometown! I wouldn't even mind getting crucified by the community. If you can't break loose from a place, crucifixion is a pretty good alternative. Drive in those nails, oh you fat-lazy-rich sons of Bushmont!

And I was influenced by the Christian Brothers, believe it or not. They spoke about the "life of a Christian" all the time. According to them, "detachment" was indispensable for the Christian if he wants to attain his "ideal" state of being. An idealist like me is a sucker for that kind of talk. "Detachment," they said, "is the indispensable condition of love. Only to the degree that self-interest is absent can interest in the good of others, or love, dominate a man's life." Good words! And how better to detach oneself than by becoming a priest?

"You can be a good Christian," said my father, "and still not become a priest."

"Maybe so," I said, "but how can you reject all worldly goods if you're supposed to succeed in business and make money?"

"It's no sin to make money. There are a lot of wealthy people around who are also good Christians."

The Rich Christians! "A contradiction in terms!" yelled Neil Ulrich, whom we had started calling The Mad Philosopher. And the richest Christians of all were the Catholics who lived in Bushmont. Their big idea of self-sacrifice was putting a five-dollar bill in the collection basket every Sunday morning. Or kneeling down in church and getting their pants dirty. Self-denial? No, if you were going to be a real Christian, there had to be more to it than that.

Neil would say to me, "You've got to decide between America and Christ!" Neil had become a strong, handsome guy with green eyes and black hair, and his favorite word was "existence." He'd say to his mother, "Mom, I exist. I exist, Mom. Do you know what that means?" And to me he'd lecture, "It's impossible for Christianity to exist in America. A complete contradiction in terms!" As a matter of fact, Neil himself was a contradiction. He loved to talk about "being" and "essence" and "love" but in the process he nearly killed people. One time he actually beat up his own parents. I had gone over to his house for dinner, and Neil got into the subject of *everything*. By that I mean his mind went all over the map. He was talking about the need for self-sacrifice, but right in the middle of his speech he said, "Mom, do you have to make so much noise when you eat?" Can you imagine a kid saying this to his mother? Neil just hated the sound of people chewing their food. It must have struck a nerve in him somewhere, like a dentist's drill. Neil slammed his fist down on the dining room table, making all the plates and the glasses fly up about a foot in the air. "I can't *stand* it!" he screamed, and in the next moment he was saying, "Soul is an intangenital [sic] elliptical process of vegetation that vibrates with sexual cognition." Christ only knows what he meant by that, but it didn't matter because he said it through his teeth. He'd say, "You've got to *feel your essence* in order to love," but he'd say it through his *teeth,* as though he were about to grab you by the throat and *squeeze* his thoughts into your mind. Maybe he was that way because he had trouble choosing the right words in order to communicate, I don't know. Anyhow, after dinner he got into an argument with his parents over this Christianity-capitalism thing, and he put up his fists and started *jabbing* at them. He always terrorized the hell out of his parents, so that they went around saying, "Yes, Neil. Right, Neil," but this time he was too worked up to be placated. He was dancing around the living room, like a boxer, and shouting.

"In America," he said, dancing about and stabbing the air with his fists, "the goal is to be *rich.*" With that, he lunged a few steps and punched his father in the stomach! No kidding! I nearly climbed out the window. "No question about it!" he yelled. "In Christianity, the goal is to *love thy neighbor.*" Smash! He slapped his mother across the face with an open palm. "We *say* we love our neighbors," he growled, and on *say* he jabbed his old man again. "But *do we?*" Another left hook, this time to his father's chin! "How can we, when we spend all our time *providing* for ourselves?" On that note, Neil went wild. The more his parents urged him to calm down, the wilder he got, until before long he actually beat up his parents, just like in a saloon in a TV western. I tried to cool him down, but he hit me, too. I swear to God, he left both his parents lying on the floor with black-and-blue marks all over them. We went out into the night air after that, and he said to me, "I *love* my parents. You know that? Whatever I am, my *being,* it comes from them. And I *love* them." Through his teeth, he said it.

As for me, I suggested to my father, "Why don't you give ten thousand dollars to the poor, and let me *work* for the money if I want to attend college?"

"I made that money for *you,* son," was the reply.

As Neil would say, "Those who *do* give lots of money to the poor can *afford* it. You don't give to the poor unless it's comfortable to do so, not in America."

And I figured he was right. I mean, to have rejected my father's money would have been to *disown* him. And not going to college was like dropping out of America.

"College," said Neil, shaking his fist at the sky, "is the

beginning of a lifelong course of self-interest."

"What do you mean?" I said.

"Well, do you think it's education for *its own sake?*"

"It's necessary to get a good job," I offered.

"That's what I'm telling you," Neil screamed as he danced around in the street and hammered the side of a parked car with punches.

But what I was saying, in the first place, was that I really was thinking about being a priest. I thought it would solve the question of living in America and rejecting worldly goods at the same time. You could spend your life doing things for other people. When I told Eddie Reilly, he said, "If you *really* want to be a priest, you should become a *monk.*"

"Why?"

"Because monks are the real thing."

"You think so, Ed?"

"Yeah. And being a monk would be pretty neat. You get to live off the land that way."

"Why don't *you* become one, Ed?"

"Nah."

"How come?"

"Too strict. And too much praying all the time."

"You think so? Is that why you wouldn't want to be one?"

"Yeah, and also because monks don't *do* anything. Not *real* monks, anyway."

Soon after that conversation, I stopped actively thinking about being a priest. If the *real thing* was being a monk, I didn't want any part of it. I wanted to be one of those cool young priests whose eyes got all glassy when you said something off-color. A young Christ hustling around, being real hip to everything and so forth. But Eddie was right. Priests aren't the real thing. At least, not the ones who were popular with adults. Rebel priests were okay, but then why didn't they quit? Maybe if they quit the priesthood they couldn't be rebels any more, I didn't know. I was pretty mixed up about it. And besides, there wasn't any rush.

6

Escaping

After sophomore year, Eddie and Ken and I decided that we had had enough of the Blessed Mother bus. Actually I was the one who initiated the move, after Joyce transferred from St. Mary's. Neil had gotten his own car and was driving her to Brookdale High every morning. And there I stood, waiting for the Blessed Mother bus with Eddie and Ken. We must have looked like an unlikely threesome, to begin with. Eddie was short and stocky, with laughing brown eyes, and he'd throw pieces of gravel at a Stop sign while we waited for the bus. A very immature thing for a high-school boy to do. And Kenny was tall and thin, like a bent piece of wire, with long black hair that curled about 360 degrees over his forehead. His face was pale and lean, and his long nose made his eyes appear more sunken than they were. I stood between them on the corner as Neil drove past with Joyce in the car. Laughing and honking their way to the high school! Well, I was jealous. And embarrassed, in a way, because neither Eddie nor Ken were very big on romance, which at times seemed to be all I thought about. Eddie was just too busy for girls, while Ken was almost a girl himself. I mean, he had grown up practically as Joyce's girlfriend. When I was little I had walked by Joyce's house many times while she and Ken were playing in her driveway. Joyce would be standing over her toy stove while Ken walked her doll carriage up and down the driveway. Whenever I'd make a snide comment, Joyce would defend him: "Shut up, David! Just get away! It's my house!" So anyway, there I stood between my two non-lover friends, and yet I was supposed to be the All-American boy! With blue eyes and freckles! Archie Andrews with light-brown hair!

So I announced **I** was going to Brookdale High School, and soon Eddie and Ken decided to make the switch with me. Not without tremendous argument from our parents, of course. But we all noticed the difference immediately. After a few weeks, girls became companions instead of either sacred temples or objects of desire. Suddenly education became a matter of thinking for ourselves, rather than of memorizing answers to prearranged questions. When I first had a test at Brookdale High, the teacher said, "Take out some sheets of paper and just write for the whole period on whatever interested you about the book."

What *interested* me? I had never even thought of it that way. Where were the questions? Why hadn't I been given some answers to memorize? What was this? My mother noticed that my marks were dropping, and she thought that the public school was leading me astray. Actually, it's just a lot tougher to think for yourself. It's difficult to explain this to some people, though. I've heard many parents say, "My son was doing very poorly in public school, but when he went to Catholic prep school his marks shot right up. Those Brothers really make them work." No, no! Work, maybe, but not *think.* I spent junior and senior years of public high school trying to crawl out of the protective, well-disciplined womb of Blessed Mother.

Also, now I was going to school with kids of different backgrounds. Jews, Protestants, Negroes. Rich kids and poor kids. See, Brookdale High covered the Village of Bushmont *and* the Town of Brookdale, which of course included the Flats. And when you start making friends with kids of other races and religions, you start seeing the paradox of Catholic teaching. The Brothers spoke of "Christian" charity, but that in itself was uncharitable. It implied that the only kind of charity was the Christian kind, and that Jews and atheists couldn't be charitable.

I asked Eddie if he thought that we had been warped by Blessed Mother, and he said no, he didn't think so. He said he didn't even know what I *meant.* He did like the public high school better, but that was because it had a shop class where he could make all kinds of stuff out of wood. Otherwise, he just hated any kind of school and laughed at everything about it.

One time I said, "Eddie, you're flunking just about everything but shop class. Aren't you worried?"

"Nope."

"Why not, Ed?"

"Because I'm going away."

While he stood outside things, I seemed to be trapped in them. Just because you denounce something about your life doesn't mean that you're free of it. I said that I hated Bushmont, yet I couldn't seem to stop getting involved in its way of life. I said I didn't believe in God any more, but I *thought* about God all the time. Sometimes the more actively you hate something, the more tied to it you become. What I didn't realize at the time, of course, was that you have to replace what you hate with something else if you want to be free of it.

Anyhow, I wanted to start looking at life a lot more. Eternity was receding in my mind. I started looking for soul somewhere else. Not in terms of aspirin or bread, but in terms of living. And if you come from the suburbs, and if you're pretty well-off and not oppressed by society like Jesus was, then you've got to look extremely hard for soul. Because Jesus Christ, whatever He was, *did* have soul. He was a Jew like Mr. Greene and got busted and they nailed Him up. He cried out and it started thundering and raining like in the movies. Society had oppressed Him, and for trying to change things, He got lynched. So if you can't go up to Communion any more to get a piece of Jesus' soul, you've got to look around for it all over again. If you're not oppressed yourself, usually you can find it in other people. When you do, you appreciate them very much. You tend to like those people, to want to be around them, to act like them, even. But still, that's not the same as finding it inside yourself. You're still empty.

7

The Dodgers and Me

So you begin to identify with people who seem to have soul, to get into their shoes, so to speak. It can be a big preoccupation. I think I even had looked for soul in the Brooklyn Dodgers, back when I was twelve or thirteen. I used to sit on the porch with a tall glass of soda and put my feet up in front of the TV to watch Roy and Jackie and Duke and Carl and Pee Wee and the rest of them. I hated the Yankees, with their clean uniforms and big stadium and world-championship title, always winning in those days. See, the Yanks *should* have been my team, because I was a winner just like them. I may have disliked Bushmont, but I knew I was pretty damn lucky. I was glad that I hadn't been born in China or India or one of those "godforsaken" places, and I also knew damn well that some people were well-off while others weren't. You grow up in a nice, established suburb, not in a sterile subdivision but in a place with lots of "character" to it, and it's like being told you've come into the world with a lucky number. I was one of the babies who had won the prize. You just accept it from the moment you're born, and rooting for the Yankees should have gone along with all of that.

I had noticed that most of my friends on Valley Stream Road were rooting for the Yanks. Eddie Reilly didn't even watch television, so I'm not talking about him. But the other guys were all Yankee fans, so in the beginning I just took the Dodgers for my team in order to be different. Also, there was really a good deal of suffering involved, and that's where this looking-for-soul business comes in. You had to like pain a little bit to be a Dodger fan.

There was something else about it, too. For me, I think it was the way the Dodgers behaved. They were sort of like a bunch of sandlot kids. We didn't have sandlots in Bushmont; we had nice, green fields of grass. And the Dodgers weren't so organized as the Yanks. They didn't have the farm teams or the money behind them. There were just those nine guys and a few extras—pitchers and batting subs—and the Dodgers nearly killed themselves every time they took the field.

They'd often do some amazing things on that crummy Ebbets Field, too. Roy would get a timely hit; Duke would hit not one, but two, homers over the fence; Pee Wee, that real little guy, would bloop one over the second baseman's head; and so on until, almost tragically, they'd lose through some unbearable series of mishaps. But when they won, they *won*. A win by the Dodgers was worth five by the Yanks, so that at the end of the season I was always ahead. In terms of feeling, not runs, nor in terms of position in the standings. It was *feeling* that I was after. The feeling of having struggled. The feeling of being a tragic hero, which means a winner even in defeat.

Why didn't the kids in the neighborhood see that? How come they were so content with the Yankees? They were always *pleased* when the Yanks won, but they never had that feeling I'm talking about. They sort of grinned and patted themselves on the back. They turned off their TV's, at the end of a Yankee game, with neither a shriek nor a moan. They just turned them off and went on with whatever they were doing. If the Yanks lost, so what? They'd win tomorrow. If they won, so what? They always won. How come my friends chose that kind of emotion over the one I'm talking about?

What puzzled me even more, though, was that our cleaning lady, Ella Washington, would always want to watch the Yankees. Now, that surprised me, because there weren't any colored guys on the Yankees. They were all white with clean uniforms and they had money and power. They weren't bums from Brooklyn.

"How can you root for the Yankees?" I asked her.

"'Cause they win," said Ella.

Poor Ella. She was getting old and I knew she lived in a shack somewhere in the Flats section of Brookdale, near the train station. I knew I was much better off than the maid, but in baseball she had a real choice. She just as easily could have chosen the Dodgers.

One time Ella was over at the house when the Dodgers weren't playing. They had lost three games in a row and were heading for worse trouble somewhere else in the country. I was reveling in the pain of their defeats. Ella wanted to watch the Yankees play, so I turned them on. I knew they'd win, but as usual whenever I watched them, I hoped they'd lose. I hoped they'd get the crap beat out of them. Naturally they breezed through nine innings to victory, and Ella said, "How d'ya like *that* for a team!" I looked at her and realized she was reacting much differently from the guys from my neighborhood. She was really excited and emotional about it, really proud. She seemed to be having the same feeling about the Yanks' victory as I always had when the Dodgers won. This disturbed me. How was Ella able to derive such a feeling from continuous and, to me, sickening victory? My parents' maid was able to have the best of both worlds: that great inner feeling *and* victory all the time. A normal, run-of-the-mill win for the Yanks was as good for Ella as an astounding, once-in-a-blue-moon win by the Dodgers was for me. I couldn't figure it out at the time.

About three years later or so, Ella switched to the Giants because her son, George, was a Willie Mays fan. Ella was scrubbing the kitchen floor, listening to a Giants game on the radio. Then she fixed me a sandwich and turned to a station that played some strange music. Ella, old as she was, started humming and swaying to the music.

I had never heard this kind of singing before. I learned soon enough that it was "rhythm and blues" or "rock 'n roll" or "soul," but at the time I didn't even know it was Negro music. I thought that some kind of wild, moving, unique white people were singing. I didn't say anything, just kept eating my sandwich and listening.

But do you know what it is, when you're young, to turn a corner and stumble onto an art form that communicates completely to you? You don't even realize that it's an art form, because it comes at you naked, so to speak. It seems completely natural, its outer form corresponding exactly to its inner content. All that beautiful pain, translated pulse-for-pulse into human sound! That was *me* they were singing about! How could it *not* be me, I thought, since I was able to love it so instantly and completely?

I was shocked when I found out it was Negro music. In one overwhelming revelation, I discovered that there existed people who had more tender pain on the tips of their tongues than I had in my whole range of feelings. When you're looking for soul, it's very easy to accept the fact that someone is smarter than yourself, or better at sports than you are, or better looking than you, but it's extremely difficult to acknowledge that other people, especially those of your own age, can feel more deeply than you can. And when you're young, it can be an impossible admission to make. I refused to accept it, but not in an angry way. As a matter of fact, I did just the opposite. If I had ever been prejudiced against Negroes, I erased the last vestige of such an attitude. I became a silent advocate of "civil rights" before I had ever heard the term. No, not really civil rights; I began to view Negroes with the eyes of a distant, desperate lover, pleading soundlessly to not be left in the emptiness out of which I was reaching.

8

James Dean and Me

During the time **I** was growing up there was a real swing away from the old conception of manliness. Maybe that was the reason why Blessed Mother Prep School seemed so unreal. The Brothers encouraged us all the time to "act like men" and they were forever "preparing you boys to become soldiers for Christ." It was a real status symbol to be on the Blessed Mother football team and to have an athletic letter in any of the sports. I think this virility thing was partly the reason why there was so much cursing at Blessed Mother. Anything to be masculine.

But attitudes were changing even at that time, because as kids we had to substitute new things for those we had learned from our fathers. As weak as my old man's war tales were, at least he had a war to talk about. And my grandfather, he'd never let me alone about the Depression and how when *he* was a young boy he was already pushing a broom on Wall Street. Okay, okay, Gramps old boy! So you're a tragic hero! I don't want to *hear* about it anymore! No, stop! I *know* you had no electricity when you were a kid. I *know* that you never got an allowance. So what are you handing *me* my monthly allowance for? Why do you put me down for something and then *contribute* to my easy situation? That was my feeling, because obviously we didn't have any world war or Depression to get worked up about. We wanted to be tragic heroes, sure, but time was running out. We were getting *old,* for Christ's sake.

And the future looked so bright it was sickening.

But then one rainy afternoon, Eddie and I went to the movies. We sat in the balcony and saw a rerun of *Rebel Without a Cause*, which I had never seen before. And there on the screen, something took place that changed my life. James Dean! Jimmy! I hadn't ever heard of him, didn't even know was Him, the Christ, the Second Coming! Here was Jesus Christ Himself in blue jeans, white T-shirt, and red windbreaker, guzzling down that fabulous bottle of milk (and pressing it against his forehead to cool off!). Yes, I was witnessing the closest thing to Jesus since Brother McKay had called himself another Christ. But Jimmy Dean, there was the real thing! All that exquisite, sensual pain! All that soul! And behold! He lived in a house not unlike mine, in a place not unlike Bushmont, with parents not unlike mine! It seemed almost impossible, but there it was.

When the picture was over I said to Eddie, "Let's stay and watch it another time."

"What for?"

"Let's just do, okay? Okay, Ed?"

"Nah, I don't wanna."

"Aw, come on, Ed."

"I got things to do. Let's go, David."

For one of the few times in my life up to that point, I actually had the motivation and willpower to resist Eddie Reilly. "No," I said. "You go ahead, if you like, but I'm watching the picture again."

"What was so good about the picture?"

"I just feel like seeing it again, that's all."

"Okay," said Eddie, shaking his head as he left the movie theatre.

The next time Eddie saw me, I was walking into his backyard with jeans, T-shirt, and red windbreaker with the collar up; and I was holding a quart-bottle of milk. I was mumbling and slouching all over his yard. I hunched my shoulders and squinted my eyes. I lay down on his ivy-covered stone wall, on my back, and shouted, "Ooooh-wheee!"

"What?"

"Oooooh!"

"Whassamatter with you?"

I was Jimmy Dean, digging the hell out of the blue sky and changing my mood every five seconds. A chuckle, a grunt, a *moan*, a whistle! I even imitated Mr. Magoo like Dean did in the picture: "Drown them like puppies, hehheh-heh." I walked around like a monkey.

Suddenly Ken Starro said, "Hey, you look a little like James Dean."

Ah! Bliss! Who said that? Kenny boy? Bless you, my son! Innocent Ken had said the magic words! I almost kissed him. But I didn't! No, I bowed my head so that my chin rested on my chest, and then I raised my eyes—my piercing eyes!—and wrinkled my forehead and—grunted!

"You do!" shouted Kenny. "You look a little like James Dean!"

I felt all the eyes observing me. I stared off into space, my head tilted, and—pouted! I had practiced in front of the mirror and had learned how to relax my lips while keeping them together so that they sort of drooped out the way Dean's had done.

"Oh, come on!" said Eddie Reilly, holding his stomach and squealing with laughter. "He doesn't look like James Dean. He looks like he's got a toothache!"

Still sulking, I squinted at Eddie and shot him my most piercing, most painful look. I gritted my teeth, making my cheekbones move in and out, producing my most tragic-butcool facial expression.

But Eddie just cracked up. I was now sitting—slumping, to be exact—on the wall in front of his house. He bent down and looked me in the face sideways. He could hardly control his laughter. He said, "Come on, Dave, give us a line from James Dean. Come on, Dave!"

I stood up, casual as hell. I kept my chin down and hung my arms limply in front of me. I squinted, wrinkled my forehead, pursed the lips, scratched the stomach and, in one small but beautiful, well-timed gesture, *pulled on my right ear lobe!* Then I put my left palm over my stomach and held out the right hand, bending forward all the while; and I said in a low voice, mumbling the words so they came out without the use of lip movements, "I don't want any trouble."

Eddie squealed and shrieked and jumped up and down like a maniac.

"No trouble, now," I mumbled, again repeating Dean's words from *Rebel Without a Cause.* "I don't want any trouble. Unh-unh."

What a performance! Why was Eddie laughing so hard? The bastard!

"James Dean!" he shouted. "He thinks he's James Dean!"

The other kids picked up Eddie's contagious laughter and soon I had dropped all the pretensions. Damn them! If only Natalie Wood lived next door! If only Sal Mineo would come by on his motor scooter! *They* would be appreciative.

I stopped pretending to be James Dean when around the Valley Stream Stinkers. The imitation was impossible to sustain, because they knew me too well. Especially Eddie, who saw right through me. He thought it was the funniest thing since my father's famous "brain damage" speech.

But I secretly went back to see *Rebel Without a Cause*

on several occasions. One of the scenes I liked best was when Dean kissed Natalie Wood. That was a kiss! I still believe it was the best kiss ever on film. The thing about it was that it contained much more feeling than the physical passion and not a bit of cheap sentiment. It was a sensual kiss, all right, but also a kind of spiritual one. The *anticipation* was so great! Before Dean moved in to kiss her, he hesitated, seeming to become almost *numb* with tenderness and painful joy. Then he tilted his head and opened those full, moist, red lips of his and nearly *swallowed* Natalie Wood's mouth. But he did it gently! He seemed to *ache* with the knowledge that he was doing a beautiful thing. What a kiss! Natalie, you can't tell me that you've ever had it so good since then!

If only I could have kissed a girl like that! And I did try, too. Many a time I opened my mouth, hesitated, went numb with tenderness and painful joy, only to be greeted unexpectedly by a familiar, gate-crashing tongue. An exquisite moment, shattered by the thrust of a virgin's oral protuberance.

The same tongue that so greedily snapped up Jesus-soul on Sunday mornings! I even took one of my crude girlfriends to see the movie, but during the big kissing scene she started giggling!

Afterwards she said, "You know what?"

I said, "What?" She was going to tell me that I looked like James Dean! Say it, baby! Go on, be perceptive! I'll even be modest!

"Don't you think," she said, "that Eddie Reilly is a bit like James Dean?"

My face must have turned white. I remember keeping my expression blank as hell. "Frankly," I said, once over the shock, "I can't agree with you less."

"But I think so," she persisted. You're through, baby!

Through! "For one thing, they both have the same kind of laugh. Real high, you know?"

"No, I don't know. I really don't."

"They kiss the same way, too," she said.

"What?"

"They kiss the same —"

"I heard you! I heard you!"

Until that moment I never knew that Eddie had *talked* to girls, much less *kissed* them. And certainly I didn't know that he kissed them like James Dean! I wanted to ask her if she used her guided-missile of a tongue when *he* kissed her, but I didn't.

Another scene in the movie that I liked was when Dean had tumbled out of his car just before it went over the cliff. He'd been in this great drag race with another guy, who was Natalie Wood's greasy boyfriend. The greasy guy was one of those hoody and virile punks who were going out of style. It was his idea of manliness to play "chicken" and so forth. Obviously he was no match for the sensitive Dean!

Anyhow, the greasy guy had gone over the cliff and Natalie was grief-stricken at the edge. Dean got up and started chuckling — sounding too much like Eddie Reilly for my comfort — but then he realized what had happened. The greasy guy was dead. Dean stood there and waited for Natalie to turn away from the edge of the cliff. And here comes the part I liked. He held out his hand. That's all! He held it straight out, palm open, and seemed to transmit the deepest feelings through his fingertips. Fantastic, the way he held out that hand! Natalie soon caught the vibrations and extended hers. Their hands kept inching closer until their fingertips touched. Explosions took place in my mind, in my chest!

And of course I went around Bushmont extending

my hand like that on every available occasion. I'd stick out my whole arm and let the vibrations go through, but it never worked out the way it was supposed to. I'd say to a girl, "Would you hand me the ballpoint pen, please?" Then I'd take a few steps backward so I'd have room to stretch out my hand like Dean did. One time the girl replied, "What's the matter, do I *smell* bad or something?" It took the poignancy out of the scene, to say the least.

But nothing could dull my enthusiasm for the Great Dean. I wished I could get to meet him and become his best friend. Here was someone just like me, but with real soul. The intangible qualities possessed by this fellow became the most important things in the world to me. Anyone who brought up the subject would immediately capture my respect and full attention. If someone said that he or she *liked* James Dean, I not only agreed but regarded it as a private victory and personal compliment. Yes, you're right! And if only you knew — that I, David Marsh, have a soul like Dean's! I have it, I tell you! It's within my grasp!

Yet the quality kept escaping me. I wore my James Dean clothes to parties and was scorned and mocked — instead of appreciated! — by the other kids. I drank so much milk that my mother had to revise her standard grocery order. I mumbled in class and was always being told to speak up. I began to look for little opportunities at home to re-create some of the scenes from *Rebel*. Anything for a chance to say, *"Mom! Dad!"* Oh, to say it the way Dean had, almost wailing and dissolving under his parents' thick-headedness!

When I learned that James Dean had died several years before, I went into a semi-trance. How could that be? But suddenly the logic of it all came to me, and I understood everything. I could see God's Plan. I wasn't brought up a Catholic for nothing, no sir. I could add up things so they made sense. Of course! Naturally Dean had died. It *had* to be that way, because there just wasn't room in the same world for *two* of us. I was destined to take up the—what? The cross? Yes, the cross! I would become the savior of young, white, middle-class America, bearing the burdens of affluence and emptiness, transmitting the vibrations of my quivering soul. Natalie, here I am! Lovers of James Dean, grieve not! Behold, He has come again!

My girlfriends, by the way, were absolutely *blind* when it came to noticing how sensitive and Dean-like I had become. I began to realize that these same girls lacked an appreciation of fine art, and that they were extremely taken up by worldly goods. Neil pointed this out to me. Like how they appreciated my secondhand car and my allowance money more than my newly acquired feelings. They didn't give a damn about the fact that I was a real, live—if fledgling—tragic hero.

And so it was not illogical that I exposed my penis to them so often. They gripped it with their cold hands—where I "lived," as the expression goes—and I, in return, transmitted my vibrations back to them. A hell of a way for the New Christ to be starting out on the road to crucifixion, but such is the truth.

It occurred to me in the midst of a smashing hand job that Christ had essentially been a politician. It was largely a matter of oratory, of obtaining mass appeal. And so, with a splat of semen into a cold female hand, I decided to go from the penis to politics.

"You've just given me a great idea," I said to the girl who had just jerked me off.

"I did?" she asked a bit nervously, as if to say, What's this idiot going to want next?

Later, I decided to forget about James Dean for the

moment and run for Student Council president at the high school. I would win the election and *then*, after taking the oath of office, I'd pull a Dean act on the whole student body! Right there on the stage, to the jam-packed auditorium, I'd hold both hands forward and mumble, "I don't want any trouble, now, no trouble." Ah, the shrieks that would follow! The moans! To be respected and loved by women and men alike! From the penis to the pulpit!

Every May the juniors elected the following year's Student Council president. I checked the history of school campaigns over the preceding five years and discovered, among other things, that they mirrored the political structure of Brookdale itself. With surprising regularity, the son of a local Republican would run against the son of a local Democrat. Of course the student elections were not as predictable as those in Bushmont and Brookdale. In both the village and the town, politics was a sacred institution steeped in nobility and tradition, the foremost tradition being that the Republicans always won. Not a single Democrat had been elected to public office in Bushmont Village since the turn of the century. A few got Town Council seats in Brookdale, but the majority was always Republican. No, the student elections weren't that rigid.

For reasons that still escape me, I asked Harold Brewster, the son of a prominent Village Republican, to put my name in nomination and to become my campaign manager. Why in hell did I go to the son of a Republican? Wasn't I a good Dodger fan, a true Brooklyn bum? I wanted to be a Democrat! An underdog! Actually there were no such labels as Republicans and Democrats in the school election, but I thought of it in that way. Soon I was surrounded almost exclusively by clean-cut Yankee fans from Bushmont. Protestants and Catholics! The sons and daughters of Democrats were mostly Jewish, it seemed to me. And as luck (good or bad, I wasn't sure) would have it, they nominated George Washington, son of our cleaning lady, to run against me. Blacks made up only ten percent of the student body, or even less. It was the first time in the high school's history that a black student had been given such an honor, and all my political research became irrelevant.

My father took a great interest in the election. Every evening at dinner he cross-examined me as to my strategy and progress. "Come on, Dad," I said one night. "It's not such a big deal as you're making it."

"Sure it's a big deal, David. Not the election itself, which I'm sure you'll win, but what it'll teach you. Build up your character. You conceivably could become President of our country one day. It's not an impossible thought. Anyway, it'll give you a sense of competition. That's the American way."

Ah, the American way! It was precisely that, or the competitive aspect of the contest, that was bothering me. I really did want to win, but I felt awkward trying to campaign against a black classmate, especially George Washington. He once sang a rhythm-and-blues song at a school prom and made me cry! George lived in the Flats with his mother (where else did Negroes live?), and was one of the few black students who came to school in a tie and jacket. Even the *white* kids seldom got so dressed up. If George were in high school today he'd be known as an Uncle Tom, perhaps, but in 1958 he was cool. He was sort of a little fellow, always smiling and full of life. He was studious and good at athletics, and immensely popular. In the Little League, my baseball team had played against the Flats team several times. George was the captain. One time he got hit in the head with a ball, and his forehead swelled out to the size of half an orange, but he didn't even cry. Yes, I had a secret admiration for him.

And guilt! Naturally, since his own mother was my parents' servant! On occasion Ella had brought George along to the house and I'd take him with me to Eddie's backyard. Anything to keep him away from my bedroom, to avoid having to show him how many toys I had! To avoid the embarrassing position of having to show George that I was probably the luckiest kid in the entire world! Even though I knew that Ella brought him over to the house precisely so he could get accustomed to the white world. Nothing was too good for her son. She worked day and night to be able to buy him the right clothes and to teach him how to operate in the white kids' society. Yes, even to the point of bringing him over on Halloween so he could meet white folks all over Bushmont, where it was unnecessary for him to put on a costume.

As soon as George Washington had been nominated, I should have dropped from the contest. Intuitively I knew there was a general sentiment that he deserved to win. My father countered this bit of campaign research by citing the racial figures: "Davey, the odds are with you by nearly ten-to-one." But the real reason why I didn't quit was that for a long while the students were apathetic. Until the last days of the campaign, electioneering was limited to displaying posters in the school corridors and passing out mimeographed literature in the cafeteria at lunchtime. Nobody seemed to care about the election, and that was fine with me.

Eddie Reilly declared that he wasn't even going to cast a vote, much less wear a button for one of the candidates. "Some best friend you are," I told him. "I'm not asking you to campaign for me or anything, but I could use your vote."

"Nope. Don't want to vote."

"Why not, Ed?"

"'Cause it's stupid."

"Stupid! You think government is stupid?"

Eddie laughed. "Yeah, stupid. What are you gonna do for me when you're Student Council president?"

"Well . . ."

I tried to think of what, possibly, I could do for Eddie Reilly. Nothing. First of all, the student government was only window dressing as an organization. It had never accomplished anything of relevance or value to the students. Not to my knowledge, anyway. It wasn't even supposed to, I don't think. It was part of our "educational process." Second, even if it did do something of consequence, it wouldn't have mattered to Eddie Reilly. It's one thing to make changes in an institution, but what can you do for someone who operates outside the institution in the first place? Eddie was going to school against his better judgment anyway, so he just regarded it as a pain in the ass to put up with. He hadn't the time to care about improving the school, because in a real sense he wasn't a part of it.

"Listen, Ed," I pleaded, "why don't you just vote in the election to help me out?"

"I'll vote for you," said Eddie, "if you promise to get me out of school when you're elected."

I laughed and slapped Eddie on the back, politician that I was. When you can't tell your best friend why he should vote for you, you're in trouble.

On the second Monday of May and with the voting to take place on Friday, the students seemed to come alive with excitement and anticipation. I don't think that any school election, before or since, has ever gained such wide interest. My big issue was the creation of a "weed wall" for smoking. George was promising to get the student parking lot enlarged. But these issues (they weren't even new ones, not by a long shot) were completely overshadowed by the singular circumstance that George Washington's skin was black.

Perhaps because I was George's opponent, I probably understood better than anyone else the phenomenon that was taking place. It wasn't a matter of civil rights. Not once did anyone say it was George's "right" to win the election. And no one said, "Vote Negro." Yet the white-student majority seemed to have approached a state of euphoria over their impending act of goodwill toward the black candidate. Instead of Republicans versus Democrats, the campaign had become more of a subtle rebellion of children against parents. By electing a black student, the kids would demonstrate, collectively, that they were more liberal and broadminded than the community in which they were growing up. A feeling of tremendous self-satisfaction was pervading the school.

The ridiculous and painful thing was that I, too, was part of this subtle rebellion, even though I was beginning to symbolize what the rebellion was against. I, too, wanted to elect a Negro as Student Council president (as a matter of fact, I voted for him). But there I was, running against him! I shared the unspoken feelings of the students who supported George Washington. And perhaps I was afraid to try my hardest. I feared that the students were viewing me (unconsciously, or silently) as anti-black, or at least as a symbol of the older generation's set of values and attitudes. Yet I also wanted to win. This was America, wasn't it? Wanting to win, not wanting to win—the resulting contradiction of emotions made me nearly impotent.

Another distressing aspect of the campaign, a warning signal of the distant unknown future, I should have seen, was that Joyce Clarkson was proudly displaying her "I LOVE GEORGE" button whenever her long, blond hair didn't fall in front of it. Joyce and I had started "going together" only a month or two before, after a long childhood of growing up as neighbors and as members of the Valley Stream Stinkers. She had gone out with Neil for a time, but claimed that the Mad Philosopher had forced her into a series of "disgusting" sexual experiments. I asked Neil about this and he merely explained, "Ah, she wouldn't blow me. Can you imagine that? The snob wouldn't blow me!" Well, yes, I could imagine that.

"She's pretty sophisticated, Neil. You shouldn't have tried that kind of stuff on her."

Neil went on to describe how he had taken Joyce's head in his hands (he used a basketball to reenact the scene) and forced it down to his crotch. "And she bit me!" said Neil. "The conceited little bitch actually bit me. I'm lucky she didn't bite it off."

Anyhow, Joyce was the closest thing to Natalie Wood that I had been able to find. This occurred to me after I observed several vicious arguments she had with her parents. I was present at one of her tantrums during which she threatened to run away from home. And since going "steady" with her I had met her several times at midnight after she had snuck out of the house following an argument. I'd drive away with her, in my secondhand car, James Dean all over again!

One afternoon in the school I pointed to Joyce's "I LOVE GEORGE" button and said, "How can you do this to me?"

"Don't confuse love with politics," she replied, squeezing my hand. How I enjoyed walking through the corridors with an arm around Natalie Wood's waist, moping and grunting with a girl who understood me! But for the time being, while she had that button over her breast, I merely walked at her side.

Still another disturbing thing was that I liked George Washington, on a personal basis. We played together on the high school baseball team, me as a second-string shortstop and George as one of three alternating pitchers. During a game in election week we sat together on the bench and joked about the campaign.

"You gonna win," George told me.

"The hell I am, Washington. Shit, you got all the girls on your side, including my girl."

Another player on the bench injected, "Bet you'd rather have 'em on your prick, Georgie."

"You guys got vulgar minds," said George, chuckling.

The voting was supposed to take place during lunch hour on Friday, after an assembly period in the morning. George and I were scheduled to address the full junior class in the school auditorium. The outgoing Student Council president, Warren W. Wilson III, was going to be moderator.

I cornered Kenny Starro on the day before the election and chewed him out for wearing an "I LOVE GEORGE" button. Kenny stood against the wall, his tight black pants wrapped about his long, thin, flagpole legs and buckled up around his rib cage. His long curl of black hair bounced around in front of his eyes and he looked up at the ceiling in despair. "Don't ask me," he said in his dramatic-sounding, high-pitched voice.

"Don't ask me why I do what I do. Please."

"Kenny, I just want to know, as your friend, why you're not supporting me in the campaign."

At this point, Neil sidled over and said, "I'll tell you why he's voting for George. Because Joyce told him to."

"Is that right, Kenny? Did Joyce tell you to vote for George?"

Kenny just nodded his head a few times. "I'm sorry, David," he said. "I really am."

"Don't cry," said Neil.

"But I don't understand," I persisted.

"Don't understand what?" Neil roared. "Kenny is beholden to Joyce. He loves her. She's his best friend."

"What about me, Ken?" I asked only half-seriously. "Aren't I your friend, too?"

"Of course you are," said Ken with emotion in his voice. "I'm so torn. Gawd, am I torn!"

"You should vote on the issues," said Neil with his teeth clenched again. "You should vote on the psychic truth in your being. As far as I'm concerned, Dave, I'm voting for you." He slapped me on the back and added, "She asked me to vote for George, too, but she wouldn't blow me!"

"Is that why you're voting for me?" I asked.

"I may not even vote!" Neil shouted. "Why should I? I can't stand this election campaigning and these stupid buttons! It's meaningless! It's shit! It makes me mad! I feel like ripping a voting booth apart!"

"Some friends I have," I said. "Not one of the Valley Stream Stinkers is on my side."

At home on Thursday night I worked halfheartedly on my speech. One minute I plunged ahead on my typewriter with a bold statement (I'm too embarrassed to repeat any of the crap), but the next minute I'd sit back and think of George, well-groomed and always smiling, a black youngster who had worked hard to get out of the depressing influence of the Flats and to be accepted despite his color. George was going to try for a scholarship to college, and being president of the Student Council would almost ensure that he'd receive it. He needed to win more than I did. Hell, I didn't need it at all.

I was an average student, while George was superior. He needed to be superior if he was even going to get to college. But did I want to yield to him out of pity?

My father was in the living room watching, of all things, *Amos 'n Andy*. I recalled how he had offered his talents as a Madison Avenue copywriter to the local Republicans of Bushmont, in one of their drab campaigns. My old man had zipped off a flood of material for them about "good government" and how the GOP ensured "stability" and "preservation of the character" of the community. After losing, the Democrats issued a statement that a baboon could win an election in Bushmont Village as long as he was on the Republican ticket. I let my father look at my speech after I had finished, and he went over it like a madman. I crossed out all his insertions the next morning. The old man would never know. His additions, in my opinion, were even cornier than my own words. He had put in stuff about all my "wisdom" and "experience" and how I was so "dedicated" to the betterment of Brookdale High School. Bullshit.

The next morning, all the juniors gathered in the auditorium to hear George Washington and me. He gave his speech first, while I waited in the wings with a frightening hollowness in my stomach. After almost every sentence by George, the students warmly applauded, and several times they burst out with cheering. George was giving a straightforward, bland kind of speech, but the kids loved him because they knew, behind it all, that here was a black kid who had managed to act just like a white one. He was simple and direct, he was inoffensive and occasionally humorous ("I burned my rear end on our coal stove last night"), and his sporadic lapses of good grammar seemed to increase his appeal.

Joyce waited offstage with me, listening intently. At that moment, for the first time, I really needed her support. Politics and love had definitely clashed. At one point she said, "George is so strong, but gentle." Oh, Natalie! That wasn't in the movie at all! *I'm* the one who's supposed to be strong and gentle, gentle but strong.

George wound up his speech to a standing ovation and my heart thundered against the inside of my chest. Yes, Natalie, and I'll bet you're thinking that his prick is bigger than mine! George walked modestly away from the podium toward me and Joyce, and she kissed him on the cheek. Hugging him, she said, "Oh, George, you were terrific!" Natalie!

My legs were weak as I watched Warren W. Wilson III stride to the podium from the other side of the stage. The outgoing Student Council president, a tall and chubby Irish fellow who loved to talk, then took the opportunity to make a speech of his own. He went on and on about the "joys of serving my school."

"And now," he said at last, "I would like to call upon the other candidate in this very exciting, very important election."

Wilson the Third was never content without overstating and distorting things. Aside from a bad case of arrogance, he was a typical student politician, always wearing a suit and tie and always dashing about as if he had the fate of the whole high school on his shoulders. He was one of those guys who always called you by your name, in every sentence! God, was I going to become like him?

I walked out to the podium, where Wilson shook my hand about twenty times. Then he did the most irritating thing. He *winked* at me. I watched him leave the stage before turning to the speech. I faced the students, looked out to the dark auditorium, and saw their blank but waiting faces. I wanted to throw away my speech and say, "Fellow students, I have decided not to ask for your votes. I have decided to ask you to vote for George Washington, instead of myself. We all want him to win. We know that by electing him we'll be setting an example for our community, for our parents and their rotten society. Why, George Washington can't even live in my neighborhood! We'll show them that *we* intend to include blacks as full partners in our society, when we grow up. This election isn't important, one way or another, insofar as the high school is concerned. The real significance of it is that we can show our black classmates that we're not like our parents, that things will be different when our generation comes of age. So I ask you: Throw your votes to George Washington!" And I might have added, "Acknowledge *me* as the leader of your rebellion!"

But I didn't say all that. I didn't, because I was scared shit. Also, I figured that George didn't need and didn't want my help. I would have spoiled things. The issue of race hadn't come up all during the campaign, so why should I be the one to inject it? Furthermore, believe it or not, I still wanted to win!

What I did do was lower my head and lift my eyebrows like James Dean. Now or never! I kept rolling my eyeballs down to the speech and then back up at the audience. I read one sentence at a time in this manner, mumbling all the way through it. I don't think that any but a handful of students heard even a word. When I finished, the whole audience was silent. Then they started giggling. I took a few steps away from the podium, to the left, and suddenly remembered James Dean's performance in *Giant,* how in a parade he had gestured to his friends on the sidelines by making a sort of wild Sign of the Cross. He had used his right hand, palm stretched out, and had brought it downward in front of his chest, sideways, and then—how splendidly!—had swept his hand from left to right as if to wipe a table. One small, spontaneous, beautiful, original gesture!

And that's what I gave the students in the auditorium as a sign that my mumbling had ended.

When I got offstage, amid a smattering of confused giggling and whispering, Joyce looked at me as if I had just contracted malaria. "David," she said, "we couldn't even hear you back here! What happened?"

"I don't want any trouble," I muttered, and walked away.

After lunch, during which time I voted for George Washington and spent thirty minutes hiding in the Boys' Room, I waited for the results of the election to come over the loudspeaker in my home room. Eddie Reilly whispered to me, "Hey—Jimmy!" I turned around and saw him grinning like a cat.

"Fellow students," came the self-assured and irritating voice of Warren W. Wilson III over the loudspeaker, "I am proud to announce the name of my successor. The winner is—"

I folded my speech inside my desk as Wilson exuberantly proclaimed George the winner by a margin of three-to-one. What relief! So what if I had made an ass of myself? More importantly, I would not become known as the guy who had denied the school its chance to elect the first Negro as Student Council president. Not that I could have prevented it; I just wanted to be on the winner's side, actually.

When I told my father about the election that evening, the old man's face seemed to change color about five times. He set his elbows on the dining room table and ran his hands through his hair.

"I can't understand it, Davey. You mean to say they voted for a colored boy over you?"

"He's a nice guy, Dad. I'm glad he won."

"Glad? You're glad you lost?"

"No, I said I was glad that *he won.*"

"The hell you are. Nobody likes to lose."

"Please don't feel bad about it, Dad."

"Why should I feel bad, son? You're the one who lost the damn thing. It's just a shock, that's all. Your mother and I were planning to take you out for dinner tonight, to celebrate."

"We can still go to dinner, Dad."

"I'll bet it was that Clarkson girl who undercut you. I saw that button on her when she was over here. I'd like to tell her a few things about loyalty. I damn well would!"

"For Christ's sake, Dad! Joyce didn't undercut me!"

"Well, what'd you do wrong?"

"Dad, I didn't do anything wrong! I lost!"

"You know what I think, David? You know what?"

"What? What do you think?"

"I think you lost because the boy is colored. I think maybe the white kids were afraid not to vote for him."

"What? *What? Afraid of what?*"

By this time, my mother had entered the room. She immediately assimilated our conversation and shuddered. That was her way of agreeing with my father, about the white kids being afraid.

"What, are you *cold*, Mom?"

"Listen," said my father, "these coloreds all carry knives, and—"

"No, Dad! George Washington doesn't carry a knife! He's our maid's son! He gets nineties in all of his subjects! He does better than I do, Mom! He's more white than me!"

"He's colored, isn't he?" my mother said with conviction.

"He certainly is," said the old man. "He's black as the ace of spades. I have a good mind to write a letter to the local paper. I don't want to take this sitting down."

"Mom! Dad! Please!" I bent down on one knee—like Jimmy Dean! Yes, I was re-creating a scene from *Rebel!* Oh, bliss! I didn't know which emotion was stronger, anger at my parents or joy at being able to be so mad at them. "Mom! Dad! Please!" I milked it for all it was worth. "Pleeeeeese!"

9

"An Actor Prepares"

When we were kids growing up in Bushmont, we had our own local pervert, named Henry the Mo. He might have been around fifty, give or take a few years, but the stories of his adventures as a molester of children were so numerous that he would have had to have been more like two hundred years old. Anyhow, Henry the Mo drove around in a shiny black Cadillac as a hired chauffeur for his own elderly mother. When driving the car alone, he'd creep up to about half a block from where we were playing basketball or blackjack or whatever, and then he'd wave or call to us. Of course, what he was doing there in the car was exposing himself. One time there were four or five of us standing around when Henry drove up and called for us to come over to the car. When we got fairly close to him, watching for any unexpected mechanical gadgets that might suddenly spring out and grab us, he swung open the car door and displayed himself to the sky. Henry the Mo! And I can still remember my mother saying, "Isn't he just the nicest man?" Right, Ma, and he's even a part-time Scoutmaster, ain't that terrific?

We all cracked up at the sight of Henry the Mo displaying himself while sitting with a chauffeur's hat on, behind the wheel of his mother's Cadillac. Then he closed the door and offered five dollars to any boy who would "ride around with me for a while." Eddie Reilly found this kind of thing so funny that he was jumping around like an Indian and yelling, "Whoop! Whoop!" When Henry raised his offer to ten and then fifteen dollars, Eddie jumped on my back and we both fell to the road laughing.

"Twenty-five dollars!" Henry called out, and suddenly we were getting into the big money. "Twenty-five," he repeated, "just to ride around with me for a while, to keep me company."

Neil whispered to me, "Let's beat him up and take all he's got."

"Oh, Gawd," moaned Ken Starro, who couldn't stand the thought of any violence.

Abruptly Eddie Reilly walked over to Henry the Mo and said, "I'd like to talk with you first, alone."

"Sure, sure!" cried Henry.

The rest of us sat on a wall nearby, straining to hear what Eddie and Henry were saying. I could see that Reilly was pumping Henry with all kinds of questions, and Henry looked a little afraid, or bewildered, which was strange. Neil and I were joking it up and yelling catcalls at Eddie, trying to get him embarrassed. Suddenly, without saying a word to us, Eddie went around to the other side of the car and got in next to Henry. Man, were we shocked at that. The two of them drove off together and Neil and Ken and I sat there wondering whether to laugh or become concerned.

"Holy shit!" Neil exclaimed. "Eddie's gone off with Henry the Mo!"

"Jesus H. Christ," I said.

We played some basketball in Eddie's driveway, waiting for him to return. Mrs. Reilly came outside at one point and asked for him, saying she wanted Eddie to fix some plumbing in the kitchen for her. He was good at that kind of thing. What were we supposed to tell her, that her son had gone off with the neighborhood pervert and at this very moment is probably performing some unbelievably obscene act in the front seat of a Cadillac? We told her we didn't know where Eddie was, but we expected—we *hoped*—that he'd be back soon.

"I wonder what they're doing," I said to Neil.

"Me too."

"Think he's in trouble? I mean, maybe we should call the police."

"I don't know, Dave. Man, I don't know."

When Eddie appeared about an hour later, we couldn't tell from his expression what, if anything, had happened.

"How's Henry The Mo?" Neil asked.

"Don't call him that," Eddie replied.

"Did you get the twenty-five dollars?" I asked.

"Nah."

"Well, what'd you *do?*" Neil said.

"Just took a ride."

We asked him a few more questions, but he just mumbled in reply. He was carving something out of wood with his pocket knife. Then his mother came outside and asked him to fix the plumbing, and he disappeared, a mystery.

What bothered me, in the days and weeks that followed, was that once again Eddie had learned something that I hadn't. Every time I brought it up he just dismissed the subject as if he hadn't heard me. Once in a while Henry The Mo would appear, but without stopping to wave or call to us. And we never made fun of him any more in the presence of Eddie Reilly.

It's amazing how much material you can collect about someone with whom you want to identify. I knew lots of guys who did that with Elvis Presley. They had every inflection down pat. There must have been a hundred imitations of Elvis walking around Bushmont, and all of them went to the high school. The funny thing was that you'd see maybe twenty guys standing and leaning around in the hallway outside the girls' gym, and not one of them would think to say, "Hey, you know what? We all look like Elvis Presley!" Can you imagine some guy saying that?

Perhaps the best imitation of Elvis Presley was performed by none other than Neil Ulrich. I must add quickly, however, that Neil's representation was unique because he didn't even *know* that he looked like Elvis. And more important, he didn't *want* to know it. In fact he hated kids to bring up the subject in his presence.

"I'm trying to be *myself*," Neil would tell me. "I sit in my room and think for three hours at a time."

"About what?"

"About my goddam *self*. My *being*. I swear to God, I'll kill the next person who calls me Elvis."

At any rate, Neil got drunk one night at a dance in the high school gymnasium, and he was persuaded to get up and sing "Love Me Tender" in front of the microphone. Somebody gave him a guitar, which he didn't know how to play, but his voice quivered and his lip curled *exactly* the way Elvis' did. The girls went crazy! What they didn't realize was that during the song, while he was saying, "Love me tender," he was actually thinking, "Fuck you, fatheads." He told me so.

Neil wasn't at all like the guys who were really *trying* to look like Elvis in one way or another. Some of them could recite his whole biography. That's what I did with Dean. I gobbled up every scrap of information I could. Whenever I went into a store I first looked for the movie magazines. I checked out the Dean photographs and stories and read them right there in the store. (I wouldn't have been caught dead with *possession* of one.) The incredible thing was that I remembered everything I read about him. Other things went right in my head and out again, but when it came to Dean my memory was photographic.

Eventually I had pieced together his entire life, it seemed, and of course I had a full wardrobe of white T-shirts, faded jeans, and assorted accessories, such as a pair of engineer boots, a faded-brown suit jacket, some bongo drums, a blue and-white striped T-shirt, a flute, a cowboy hat, a pair of eyeglasses without the lenses, and so forth. Dean had real long hair which he combed straight back. He had a great head of hair. So I grew my hair long, too, and in the morning I would spend an hour trying to keep it in place. By eleven o'clock all my hair was standing straight up, about a foot high. I had to keep sweeping my hands back over it to keep it down, and I had to be careful not to run too fast or jerk my head too abruptly, because then the hair would flop forward completely and blind me. It was a terrific source of aggravation, but I must have felt that it all was worth the effort.

"What's your opinion of James Dean?" I asked Eddie.

"Eh."

"You don't like him?"

"Well, I guess he's a fairly good actor."

A *fairly* good actor! I dropped the subject, unable to figure out Eddie Reilly's mind. But I did start thinking about something very obvious that hadn't occurred to me before. Of course! James Dean was an *actor*. He wasn't really a middle-class guy with parents like mine and so forth. When he was alive and in those pictures, he was a *professional actor.* A dedicated artist! How obvious, how simple!

"What would you think," I asked Eddie on another occasion, "if I told you that I might become an actor?"

"You? An actor?"

"Yeah, me. What's so funny?"

"Like in the movies?"

"Yeah, idiot, like in the movies!"

"I'd say you were kidding, Dave old boy. Either that or you've gone nuts."

"Now, what makes you say that? Hunh?"

"Well," said Eddie, chuckling, "I certainly wouldn't pay any *money* to go see you."

"Why not? Sure you would."

"Whaddya mean? I *know* you. I *see* you all the time, in *person.* Why would I pay to go see you in the movies?"

"Well, forget about yourself, Ed. What about in general?"

"Look, David, you're *not* gonna be an actor, so—"

"Yes! Yes I am! I *am* gonna be an actor!"

"You?"

"Yeah, me! What the hell's so goddamn funny?"

"An *actor?*"

"Yes! I'm gonna be an actor! Can't you understand the English language, Reilly?"

"Oh, come on!"

"You'll see, Eddie! I'm serious!"

"Stop! It's too funny!"

"Quit that laughing, will you? Can't you be just a little bit serious?"

"No! Please! Stop talking! You're killing me!"

At this point, Eddie was rolling around on his lawn, and I jumped on top of him to get him to stop laughing. I even hit him a few times in the chest, but that only made him laugh harder. He was a small guy but he had a solid body. I was always surprised to find how strong he was. His neck was real thick and I grabbed it with both hands, unable to encircle it completely. Eddie held my wrists and wrenched my hands from his neck. Strong as hell. I was looking down at him and he was laughing like crazy while the tensions in our arms built up. Suddenly I had an inexplicable urge to kiss him. I almost did, but then I rolled to the side, stood up, and made the feeling go away.

"Laugh all you like," I said, "but I really am going to be an actor. I've decided."

But what was an actor? In the absence of any practical knowledge, I began to make my own definitions. An actor: one who acts. A person who is a professional being-in-action. As opposed to a passive person. That was it! James Dean was a person in constant action. He was alive. Honesty! Simplicity! Spontaneity! He was alive, and therefore, acting was living! That's what I wanted to be: a live person instead of a dead one. To be alive! How simple, how corny, how easy, but how true!

It sounded great, but it's kind of difficult to go around repeating to yourself, "I'm alive! Hey, I'm living! Don't bother me, everybody, I'm too busy being in action! Whoo!" You can get all worked up that way if you're not careful. You can work yourself into a frenzy and wind up a little dizzy. I spent about one week being "alive" and nearly wound up in the nuthouse. I went around digging the sky and trees and the ground, and everything in sight. I laughed so hard at the stupidest things that people thought I was plastered. I couldn't sit still. By the end of the week I was so tired from all that "living" that I just had to take a rest. And besides, I had nothing to show for it except a headache from constantly bulging my eyeballs.

And so, I began to think that "living" for a living was an occupation that had to be worked for, gradually, like any other goal. I listed the various periods in James Dean's lifetime of twenty-three years—his childhood in Indiana, a little bit of college and some attempts to break into Hollywood films; and then, the plunge into New York City's jungle of a theatre world, where a man could be swallowed up, never to be seen again, or raised to the heights of artistic recognition. The route to Hollywood was through Broadway. Dean had gotten into the Actors Studio, where *his* idol, Marlon Brando, had learned his craft. Delving into this history, I learned that the Studio had grown out of the Group Theatre of the thirties, which in turn had its roots in the Moscow Art Theatre (I don't claim this to be an accurate history, but it's the way in which I thought of these things). And the foundation of all this, it seemed to me, was the "method" school of acting enunciated by Constantin Stanislayski in his great book, *An Actor Prepares.*

Have you ever wanted so badly to find a book that you actually consider breaking into the library on Sunday because it's closed that day? Could I go on existing another twenty-four hours without it? And all Sunday night? I felt like an addict in need of a fix. I wanted to get that book and *inject* it into my veins. Never mind that I hadn't the vaguest idea of what might be *in* it—I wanted what I thought that book could do for me, simple as that.

On Monday morning I took Natalie Wood-Joyce Clarkson to school and then, when we got inside the building, I pretended to have forgotten something out in the car. I raced to the parking lot, got in the old "short" and drove like a speedster to the Bushmont Public Library. Some kind of inspirational song which had just hit the Top Ten was on the radio, and that made me drive even faster. Christ, what was the hurry? I was behaving as if I didn't have any time left, as if the world couldn't wait any longer—the sands were trickling out of the hourglass in my mind! to music!—and when I got to the library it was only eight forty-five, or fifteen minutes before the old ladies came to open it up.

A quarter of an hour! As I marked time, it seemed like five hours. The only thing I wanted to do, or that I had the urge to do, was whack off right there on the library steps. Honestly, that was the only thing I was capable of in those fifteen minutes. But I didn't do it. I figured I might have such a powerful orgasm that the little-lady librarians would find me dead, sprawled out under the "Book Return" slot in the library door.

Once inside, I had to wait for them to turn on the lights. They must have wondered what kind of fantastic book they had that could make a teen-age kid storm the library like in a holdup. All right! Everybody freeze! I want that book, ladies! Hand it over!

But I went stealthily to the index cards and looked through the "A" drawer. There it was: *An Actor Prepares.* My heart began to pound as I climbed the stairs to the library's second floor. Had some other kid beaten me to it? Would it be out? Was there another budding Dean-Christ in Bushmont? God, let the book be there! I found my way to the stacks and scanned the numbers and the titles. At first I didn't see it. I went right past it and almost sank to my knees in fear. Somebody's taken it out! Eddie Reilly! Eddie, I thought you were my friend! I pictured him sitting down in his basement, *pretending* to fool with his model trains while actually studying *An Actor Prepares.* But then I spotted the book out of the corner of my eye, and I grabbed it off the shelf, slamming it against my chest and hugging it. The Bible! The Old Testament! I didn't even stop to look inside the thing.

I went downstairs on a pair of shaky legs and almost collapsed on the librarian's desk.

I hadn't noticed before, but sitting behind the desk was Mrs. Browning, a friend of my mother's from the Bushmont Women's Club. I put the book down in front of her as gently and casually as I could. The trouble was, I had to give her my library card and she saw my name. Caught in the act.

"David Marsh?"

"Yes, ma'am."

"Why, I believe I know your mother."

"Really?"

"Mildred, right?"

"Yes, ma'am."

"Well, tell her that Mrs. Browning says hello."

We talked for a few minutes about how my mother didn't look her age (score one for Mrs. Browning, I think), and somewhere in there I had to explain why I wasn't in school.

I made up something about being on a "special assignment" to the library, and that got her off my back. But then she picked up my book and examined it as though she were holding a rare stone.

"Mmmmm," said Mrs. Browning. "Are you preparing to become an actor, David?"

She said it with a wry smile, as if she knew everything that was on my mind, as if, by virtue of her age and the fact that she was a librarian, she knew all the subtle, psychological reasons (if there were any) why I was taking out this particular book. I lied about having to make a report of it for English class, and she said that *she'd* read it herself and hoped that I'd "enjoy" the book as much as she had.

Enjoy? Here I was on the brink of opening a book that would *change* my *life,* it might even change my appearance after one sitting, who knows, yet this soft-spoken, sweetly smiling, stupid woman had already read it, and what the hell had it done for her? Nothing! I gave her a painful James Dean squint. JUST GIVE ME THE BOOK, MRS. BROWNING. I'M NOT READING IT FOR "ENJOYMENT," IF YOU MUST KNOW. I'M GOING TO FOLLOW ITS PRESCRIPTION TO THE LETTER. OBVIOUSLY, IF YOU HAVE ALREADY READ IT, YOU DIDN'T TAKE IT SERIOUSLY ENOUGH, OR ELSE NOW YOU'D BE SITTING THERE LOOKING LIKE A FEMALE MARLON BRANDO.

What I can't stand is when a person who has read an inspirational book *before* I have, especially if it's a book that I think will *change* me somehow, and when this person says I should read it because it's got the "key" to life and whatnot; because the person who has already read it never seems a bit different. SO YOU'VE FOUND THE ANSWER TO EVERYTHING, THEN WHY AREN'T YOU A GODDAMN NEW HUMAN BEING? It's like watching people coming out of a movie that you're standing in line for. They're coming out, and you're about to go in. You watch their faces, to see if this great movie you've heard about has maybe *done* something to them, but usually their faces are blank, or they're smiling, or if you listen to their conversation you find out that they're talking about anything *but* the movie. Changed their lives? Not likely. The theme of the movie might have been "Peace on earth" but the whole damn crowd is pushing and shoving to get out of the theatre. A bad omen, indeed, that Mrs. Browning had read and enjoyed *An Actor Prepares.*

"We were excited as we waited for our first lesson with the Director, Tortsov, today ..."

So began *An Actor Prepares.* Excited? God, I was so feverish that I read the first sentence all over again, just in case I had missed anything between the lines. A tingling sensation went through me and then I plunged into this Book of Books. I could hardly read fast enough, yet I made sure to absorb every word.

"In the soul of a human being," I read (and as a former Captive Catholic that word "soul" still raised the hair on my arms), "there are certain elements which are subject to consciousness and will. These accessible parts are capable in turn of acting on psychic processes that are involuntary."

What? Say that again?

The actor's job, I read, "is not to present merely the external life of his character. He must fit his own human qualities to the life of the other person, and pour into it all of his own soul. The fundamental aim of our art is the creation of this inner life of a human spirit ..."

Was I getting this right? Could it be true? Could there exist a profession which had as its "fundamental aim" the *creation of an inner life of a human spirit?* In my father's work, he created the corny words for advertising commercials. If young men unconsciously compete with their fathers, then that's what I was doing; and from my point of view I was creaming him.

It all sounded so wonderful. With every word I thought of James Dean, whose "inner life" was so visible on the screen. I began to realize that it was this ability of Dean's that I was shooting for, this ability to make his mind race with thoughts, his soul swirl with feelings, while keeping his body perfectly still.

"Our aim is not only to create the life of a human spirit, but also to *express it in a beautiful, artistic form."*

I put the book down and looked in the mirror. An artistic form?

"You must be very careful in the use of a mirror. It teaches an actor to watch the outside rather than the inside of his soul."

Agh! I shrank from the mirror in guilt. But then I read the marvelous story of how the Director told this girl to go up on stage to find a brooch which had been stuck in the curtain. She dashed on stage and *pretended* to look for the brooch. Aha! She was trying "to represent the general tragedy of the situation," but had overacted terribly and, in the end, forgot all about the brooch.

Then the Director did a great thing. He told her to go back onto the stage to find the brooch, this time warning that if she didn't find it something awful would happen. She'd be kicked out of the acting school. See, he was throwing out what he called the "Magic If," which gets you to believe in a fictitious set of circumstances.

Immediately the girl's face became intense and she glued her eyes on the curtain, trying to find that goddamn brooch. Instead of beating her breast and screaming, she muttered as if to herself, "Oh, where is it? I've lost it." See, this time she was *really* upset, whereas beforehand she had only pretended. "*You merely sought to suffer for the sake of suffering.*" Aha!

"Fix this for all time in your memories: *On the stage there cannot be, under any circumstances, action which is directed immediately at the arousing of a feeling for its own sake.* To ignore this rule results only in the most disgusting artificiality. *When you are choosing some bit of action, leave feeling and spiritual content alone.* Never seek to be jealous, or to make love, or to suffer, for its own sake. *All such feelings are the result of something that has gone before. Of the thing that goes before you should think as hard as you can. As for the result, it will produce itself."*

As I read on, I discovered a theory of acting that was, to me, a paradox in some respects. See, one of the reasons why I wanted to become an actor was so I could express a whole lot of deep emotions. My actual desire was not to *really* feel pain, but to enjoy expressing it and to have the appearance of suffering. I wanted to watch myself undergoing all these great emotional experiences. But if you're supposed to be thinking as hard as you can about the *causes* of the suffering, you can't very well enjoy it.

Yet Stanislayski offered enough incentive for me to accept the paradox without further question. If I had to really feel pain and despair (in addition to their opposites), then so be it. That's life, and so forth. Indeed, it *was* life.

"Every person who is really an artist," I read, "desires to create inside of himself another, deeper, more interesting life than the one that actually surrounds him." Well, then, I figured, I *must* be an artist, because that was precisely what I wanted to do, even if I did never meet Eddie Reilly at midnight at the bridge.

I spent the whole summer between junior and senior years of high school reading and digesting *An Actor Prepares*, allotting a week to each chapter. In that week I'd read over the chapter once per day and make a list of things to work on. I really was totally absorbed in the thing, and at the same time I was looking way ahead to the school play in the winter of our upcoming senior year.

Another book I picked up and started using was called *To The Actor*. This book, written by Michael

Chekhov, had a lot of specific activities that I could perform in my own room, and I did them regularly every night before whack-off time.

"By means of the suggested psychophysical exercises, the actor can increase his *inner strength,* develop his abilities to *radiate* and *receive,* acquire a fine sense of *form,* enhance his feelings of *freedom, ease, calm* and *beauty,* experience the significance of his *inner being. ...*"

And so I am panting, *lusting* for my inner strength, but what was it that drove me so hard to become a man of feeling? Was it because of an overwhelming awareness that I had everything else *but* feeling? I don't mean to say that I was a cold person, no; but I certainly hadn't any great depth. Not a line of experience on my blue-eyed face! Oh, to be screwed up! To be psychologically twisted and wracked with unrelieved pain and suffering and even guilt! And then to rise above it, scars showing for all the world to see!

Judging from my father's virtually unlined face, there was no assurance that with age would come great depth of character. In fact, just the opposite destiny was looming. The prospect was one of more flesh around the middle and on the face, of an increasing *lack* of involvement and emotional conflict. To grow older and richer and more comfortable! To become sunburned on the golf course and windburned on Long Island Sound! To become satisfied! To become unsatisfied with satisfaction! No, no no! I was *already* all of these things, the boy-product of every striving in America's lifetime. They could make a statue of me and future historians could look at it and say, "This was the American Dream as it looked in flesh and blood. He had everything on his side; God, skin-color, money, the future, eternity." Adam might have been kicked from the Garden of Eden, but America had striven for two centuries to return him in the person of David Marsh. Yes, I was the New Adam! And anyone who knows his history can tell you that aside from heaven, the Garden of Eden is the most boring, unstimulating place ever dreamed up in the mind of men; and Adam is the shallowest, most superficial and most featureless creation of all. No wonder he ate the apple! Anything to get *out* of the Garden, to get a taste of life! Maybe it wasn't an apple at all, maybe he *masturbated* to get himself shoved out the gates, or maybe Eve jerked him off! Maybe that's why I had been whacking off all that time, to get at least partially out of the Garden, if not out of Bushmont Village.

Let me try to be more accurate, though: it's not the Garden of Eden that's so bland, per se, but our friend Adam. He could *blame* the Garden for causing him to rebel against it, but he still couldn't get away from his own inner weaknesses. And this is what I'm talking about. I may have been dissatisfied with my comfortable environment, and I probably blamed it for my own inner shallowness, but how could I run away from myself?

For example, we really had a lot of great people living in Bushmont, for all its image as a bedroom-type of community. I mean, many of the big homes were owned by people who had come from all kinds of different places and backgrounds. No blacks living in the village, but a hell of a lot of people who at one time or another in their lives had been poor. So to them, Bushmont was a great place, because they brought something of their own selves to it. Fine! Swell! But as I've remarked before, I was already there, from the beginning! How could I bring something to it? I hadn't *been* anywhere else, hadn't *done* anything of heroic proportions. I was, in fact, *part* of the environment. With no more substance than the tree in our front yard!

Well, that's what I was trying to correct, in my own peculiar style. Psychophysical exercises! Masturbation! Yes, whacking-off exercises, during which I did *not*, as may be presumed, dream of fucking beautiful girls. No, I dreamt of throwing footballs for seventy-yard completions, of hitting the first ball clear out of Yankee Stadium (as a Dodger in the World Series, of course), of being a nomadic bum wandering across continents—and if I did dream of sex, it was usually as a female. Perhaps I was just trying to throw off whatever I could blame for feeling imprisoned, and perhaps my maleness was just another lining of bars to be stripped away. I often dreamt of being made love to—being *manhandled—by* Eddie Reilly. Why? Well, I'm no authority, but it's obvious that if I loved anyone it was him. And also because I figured that females had, at least they seemed to have had, more sensitivity than guys. I suppose I was envious of Eddie's being called "cute" by the girls, because I knew that they meant he was somewhat like them, that he was *lovable,* that he inspired emotions of love . . . while still being totally male, and strong. Me, I had to become a girl, at least in my dreams, to compete with him. And at the same time, to share him.

So there in my bedroom, I tried to make myself more lovable (to myself?). I read where Michael Chekhov says that the actor must "consider his body as an instrument for expressing creative ideas on the stage, *must* strive for the attainment of complete harmony between the two, body and psychology."

But my interpretation of this ran amuck somewhere. Someday I just might sue Charles Atlas for giving me a pair of oversized tits. I wouldn't say that I'm *deformed* or anything, but I'm certainly not proud of the way my boobs hang over my stomach the way they do even now. A good deal of the blame has to be placed squarely in the massive lap of Charles Atlas. I sent for all of his lessons and started in on what he called nervous-tension exercises, along with my Stanislayski and Chekhov work. No, *dynamic* tension, that was it. You press the fist of one hand into the palm of the other, in front of yourself, and one side of your chest gets quite a workout. It sort of quivers all over. You have to alternate this exercise from one fist to the other, or else you'll come out with one tit larger than another. I didn't make that particular mistake, but in later years my barrel chest has become rather flabby.

I suppose, though, that the Atlas phase was an error on my part. Charlie had wanted to help guys to prevent bullies from throwing sand in their faces, but that wasn't my objective, and I should have known better. But you start on a Self-Development kick within the walls of your own room, and you're bound to make all kinds of mistakes. It's not healthy. In Chekhov's book it said that the body of an actor "must absorb psychological qualities," that it "must be filled and permeated with them so that they will convert it gradually into a sensitive membrane, a kind of receiver and conveyor of the subtlest images, feelings, emotions and will impulses." And me, I almost wound up needing a bra.

10

Making Choices

Can anyone doubt that also during the summer I was a lifeguard at a local beach club? I mean, could David Marsh been anything *other* than a lifeguard at some point in his life? There I was, sitting up on my highchair in the sand, being admired, so I thought, by all the little Christian white girls with their varying degrees of tender skin. What a bootiful child! They *seemed* to admire me, but how often did I ask one for a date and find out what they *really* felt? I'd pick up the girl at her house and, while waiting for her to appear, sit in the living room and talk with her daddy. And she would come downstairs and stand there looking *down* at us, waiting politely but with superiority while her daddy and I finished our little man-to-man chat. He would be saying, "Yes, and so a good liberal-arts background is what the companies are looking for these days. Good long-range thinking, young man." What her daddy was really saying, however, could have been translated to, "David, you're on your way to becoming just like me, to becoming just like this little girl's daddy. Keep up the good work, son." And the girl would be smirking, behind that mask of a fun-frolic face, because she thought her daddy was a big square, see. She instinctively knew that her mother was sexually unsatisfied (not to mention emotionally) with this father of hers, no matter how many babies were produced, no matter how many home movies they made, and she could see that I was growing up to be just like her daddy. The girl probably could see a dismal future with no more than three and a half orgasms in it, and so when we got out of that house, man, she was looking for some *action*. She was looking for excitement, and she wasn't finding it in me, lifeguard or not. I was simply her front man, so to speak, her means of getting out of the house. A pimp! Most of the girls went through at least one stage (Joyce Clarkson, whose goal was to marry an international billionaire, went through several of them) where they sought out the biggest hoodlums in Brookdale, even if only to be seen with one of those greasy cats, and to be able to give the *impression* that they were getting the daylights banged out of them. Which some of them were. One girl actually phoned me up and said, "David, could you call for me tonight at around eight-thirty and drive me to the bowling alley? I have **a** date with Studs, but my parents won't let me see him. . . . Thanks, David, you're a dear."

A pimp!

Oh, yes. I also *modeled* on several occasions that summer. My father, noting my interest in acting, arranged through his advertising agency for me to pose for several color photographs which subsequently appeared in a bunch of women's magazines. I forget what the ads were selling, but there was no doubt that I was being featured as the All-American boy. I posed in bathing suits and in ties and jackets and in sweaters and ski parkas, usually with a shit-eating grin on my face. Not a thought in my brain—and worse, not an emotion in my gut! Young Adam in the Garden!

In the fall of senior year I joined the bowling team, and I'll bet I was one of the first people to use the Stanislayski Method while flinging a ball down the alley. I'd get up there to bowl and I wouldn't throw the ball until I *felt* it. My teammates would yell at me to hurry up and *roll the fucking ball, will ya!*

"I'm not motivated yet," I'd think to myself as I faced the lineup of pins at the end of the alley. *If I don't get all those pins down in this one turn,* I would think, *I'll be shot in the back immediately.* The "Magic If" really seemed to work. I actually started bowling better than ever before. I aimed at those pins as if it were a matter of life or death.

When I thought about this technique later, I figured that Eddie Reilly probably used the "Magic If" as a natural part of his daily living, although I'm sure *he* didn't think of it that way. The whole Stanislayski Method was geared to making people become like Eddie. I'll bet he could have been a great actor, but of course it never would have occurred or appealed to him.

But it must have been sheer masochism on my part to have joined the bowling team. Here was a sport unrivaled, except perhaps by chess, in its lack of a following. *Following?* We were lucky if anybody knew that a bowling team *existed* at Brookdale High. Small wonder, then, that my breakup with Natalie Wood, alias Joyce Clarkson, occurred in the wake of our Fall Championship Match.

I had invited Joyce to the match, mistake number one, and proceeded to bowl three games averaging just below a hundred, error number two. Bad enough that I was a member of a minor sports team, but worse that I bowled so poorly the one time that Joyce was there to watch me.

You have to imagine what it's like to play a bowling match at four o'clock on a Tuesday afternoon. The Brookdale Bowl, a monster-child of the technological-leisure-class society, was empty except for the man at the counter, who looked as if the loneliness of the place had entered his brain like a dull chisel. We were playing the other team on lanes 32 and 33 or thereabouts, which meant we were located in the middle of nowhere. No cheering crowds, either; no band, no cheerleaders, no scoreboard, no invigorating smell of dry autumn leaves—just a large, depressing echo-chamber with rows and rows of empty, polished bowling lanes. The five of us from Brookdale High—Yay, team!—were wearing our gaudy, glossy orange shirts with black lettering, and the other five guys were wearing their gaudy, glossy gold shirts with purple lettering. What did we put on such uniforms for, I wonder? I mean, who ever came to watch us play? Honestly, nothing could have been less exciting, romantic, or spectacular than the sight of ten pale-skinned guys with neon shirts competing against each other in that vast cavern of waxed bowling lanes and impersonal pin-setting machines. I imagined each lane as the long tongue of a savage beast.

And there sat Joyce Clarkson, our one spectator, dragging on her Marlboros, flirting with the opposition, and clucking *her* tongue. Joyce, who was a bronze cheerleader for football games on those glorious Saturday afternoons! Joyce, who had ridden shiny black horses from the age of three! Joyce, who probably associated bowling alleys with the Mafia! I should never have invited her. She sat behind us on one of those seats that looked as if it had been stolen from a movie theatre. I'd get up to bowl and then sit down again with the fellows, turn my head, and say, "Joyce, I should have gotten that spare, you know?" You know that, baby? Ah, the wooden smile in response! As if to say, "When you're forty years old, David, you'll probably bowl every Tuesday night with the fellows, drinking beer and missing spares." I couldn't concentrate on my Magic If for the life of me. At one point I even hit the ball against my leg, causing it to ricochet into the adjacent lane. Great laughter, much embarrassment on my part. I'm sure that bringing Joyce to my bowling match was a major factor in our separation.

Anyway, I drove her home that evening (after we lost the match) and we talked in her back porch, where recently I had been trying The Magic If during our lovemaking. I was still wearing my glossy orange shirt, which now had two huge ovals of sweat radiating from the armpits. Joyce was tearing into me: "You mope, you slouch, and you have no ambition."

"What do you mean, no ambition? I'm gonna be an actor!"

"That's not ambition, it's obsession. Or better, it's delusion."

"Why do you say that? What gives you the right to say I'm deluded?"

"David, you're not somebody that people would take the trouble to go see in the movies. It's nothing against you personally, but movie stars have certain *qualities* that *make* them stars. Like basketball players are *tall*. It's their *tall*ness that makes them good players. You can't just *want* to be a basketball player."

"Sure you can, Joyce."

"Not if you're four feet tall, you can't."

What she was saying, if I understood correctly, was that when it came to personality-potential for the movies, I was a shrimp. "Who's talking about basketball?" I demanded. "I want to be an actor. Not necessarily a star, just an actor. It doesn't matter if I'm tall or short, or skinny or fat, or old or young. Outward things don't make any difference."

"What does, then?"

"Inner things."

"Like what? Your digestive tract?"

"Come on, Joyce, don't you know the difference between inner and outer?"

"All I know, David, is that you're too *average* to be in the movies. You're not *special*."

"Everybody's special, stupid."

"Oh, really? Then why isn't everybody in the movies?"

"Because not everybody *wants* to be."

"I told you, David—just wanting to be something doesn't make you become it."

"How do you know? I'm talking about art, for Christ's sake. Maybe you are what you *think* you are. How about that?"

"That's delusion, like I said in the first place."

"Maybe," I countered, "art itself is a delusion."

"David, I can't continue this discussion."

"Listen, Joyce, take James Dean—"

"*Take* him! If I hear his name one more time I'll scream! *Take* him! I've got him for a boyfriend!"

"All right, lay off, will ya? What I'm saying is that James Dean, if you think about it—"

"Which I don't."

"If you think about it, he was an average guy himself. I mean, he wasn't any extra-special person as far as outward appearance goes. He was just a normal guy if you broke him down, feature by feature."

"This is ridiculous, David. So what if you chopped him up, feature by feature?"

"So that's what I'm telling you. Here was a common, ordinary guy, who turned out to be somebody really exciting, through *art*. Because of what he was *inside* of himself, that showed through."

"And just what's inside *you* that's gonna show through all of a sudden, when the camera gets on you?"

"I've got feelings, dammit!"

"So does *everybody*."

This was the kind of conversation that drove me nuts. I hated Joyce for not being on my side. A girl was supposed to give you encouragement, to *believe* in you, or at least pretend to. But maybe that was already becoming old-fashioned, I don't know. It was getting harder all the time to find a girl who lied to you about how wonderful you were. The girls were becoming too honest about everything. They were almost as strong as the guys, in a sense. Even stronger. My father's generation had had it easy in that respect. All the girls thought the guys were so damned great because they had gone off and defended our country and so on. But what do you say to a girl who's gone through exactly what you have, and who constantly reminds you of that fact, one way or another? I mean, what could distinguish my life's experience up to that point from Joyce's? And she and I knew the future, too. We knew that nothing would happen in the coming years that would distinguish our histories, either. We'd both go to college, we'd both get jobs. Male? Female? Those were becoming merely words. I swear, there was a whole lot of adjusting to do.

Don't misunderstand me, though—I *liked* girls to be honest and truthful. I knew it was a good thing and so forth, but it was kind of hard on the ego, that's all. This was especially so in the case of Joyce Clarkson who, despite her critical intelligence and similar tough-minded capabilities, wanted it both ways. I mean, she could cry on the spot. After she asserted *her* masculinity, she'd reverse the roles back again. "If you're really set on becoming an actor," she said, "then I think our relationship had better end, right now."

"Why?"

"Because you'll fail. You'll spend years and years auditioning, and you'll wind up begging in the streets."

"So what? At least I'll have tried. I'll have struggled for something important to me."

"Well, you go ahead, David. But don't expect me to go along with you. Struggle all you like, but don't drag me into it. That's not fair."

"Fair? Fair to whom?"

"To me."

"How about to me?" I demanded. "You're not being fair to me."

"I have a right to expect that you'd earn a decent living, don't I?"

"I don't know, Joyce. Besides, it's a little early to be thinking about all that."

"It's not too early to know that I want a family someday. Children, a house, and—"

"And what? A two-car garage?"

"Security! I know how much you dislike that word, David, but I have a right to expect that the man I marry will *care* for me, that he'll *provide* for me, and—"

"Oh, you do, eh?"

"Yes, I do."

This girl may have looked a bit like Natalie Wood, but only from a distance. Oh, to find a girl like the one in *Rebel*! One who didn't give a damn about material goods! One who would love me for my sensitivity, my soul! I had visions of her going off with some cold-blooded insurance adjustor, some insensitive Wall Street guy—a Yankee fan!—and living in a little white house in Bushmont, with nineteen children. I envisioned myself as a great actor who had finally made it after ten long years, and of her coming backstage with her blank-faced husband after seeing me in a show, after *weeping* over my performance. She'd come to the door of my dressing room and look at me with water-filled eyes, wishing that she had waited for me, that she had put her faith in my dreams instead of marrying Clark Kent or whatever his name would be. I would stand there and even get a little wet-eyed myself, fully understanding her misfortune. After all, I would think, glancing in the mirror at myself, look what she's lost! She sacrificed feelings for security and wound up with a boring, hateful life!

"It's your choice," I said with conviction. "You have to decide what you value most in life."

"I value common sense, among other things."

"Well," I shouted, becoming almost giddy with the thought of how right I was, of how daring and adventuresome I was being, "then you certainly shouldn't stick with *me*! I'm a bad bet! The odds are poor! If common sense is your guide, then you'd better break loose from me right now!"

Yes, I enjoyed the whole thing. How sweet to be rejected! How beautiful to have sentiment on my side! I imagined that we were playing the final scene of a movie, with the audience pulling for me every step of the way. I might as well have been saying, "Don't bet on the Dodgers. It's not common sense. They'll probably lose. Of course if you *did* bet on them, and if they *happened* to win, then you'd really have something going for yourself. Even if you *lost* you might be better off. But go ahead, bet on the Yankees. Go on, be secure!"

We broke up amid tears and slobbering kisses (memories of all those nights in the back seat of my car must have counted for *something* in the way of good old romance), but she managed to get in the final word. "David," she said, "I hope you become an actor. I hope you become a big star, just like James Dean. And I also hope you'll learn to love someone other than yourself."

Same to you, Natalie!

It was kind of interesting to see what new people we'd start going out with. I began dating this Jewish girl named Sandra Klein. Needless to say, I felt as if I were doing something really courageous and adventuresome. A blue-eyed Catholic boy dating a Jewish girl! By the way, I had been told that Jewish girls really "put out" a lot and so forth, but Sandra Klein squelched that one for me, proving the old point that you can't generalize. The closest I got to anything exciting was a dry-hump or two while dancing at a party with the lights out.

But my little adventure turned out to be nothing, absolutely *nothing*, compared to what Joyce now was doing. I began noticing that she was walking through the corridors a lot with black kids. Wow! She even ate at their lunch table in the cafeteria! And smoked with them in the parking lot! And she informed me, with a ring of pride in her voice, that she actually had attended *a party in the Flats*. This was astounding news. I was extremely impressed, even jealous.

I should mention here that many of the black kids — George Washington excepted — had become very cocky and arrogant, now that we were in the twelfth and final grade of high school. They'd come up to you in the hall and say, "Hey, man, got any spare change?" or "Hey, baby, gimme a weed." They seemed to do it just to make you feel embarrassed, or guilty. Naturally I always reached in my pockets for whatever they wanted, because I *was* embarrassed and guilty.

I figured I understood why they were so cocky and arrogant. Until senior year, there had been a feeling that everybody was equal, almost, since we were all together, going to the same school; but now that illusion was disappearing. The black kids weren't taking the same courses that we were, because they weren't going to college. The principal and the dean and the teachers were carrying on about college so much that you'd have thought the end of the world was coming—and this must have made the "colored" kids wonder about things. There were really two schools in one building, one for the rich and one for the kids who didn't have any future.

Beyond that, I also felt that I, personally, had a lot of rapport with the black kids. Of course I probably didn't have *any* rapport with them, but for some reason I *thought* I did. Maybe because I listened to blues music and rooted for the Dodgers, God knows.

(The only white kid from Bushmont who *did* have genuine rapport with black guys was Eddie Reilly, who also didn't have any future.)

I remember telling my parents, with an air of great superiority, how *enriched* I was because I was going to school with black students. And I remember this one basketball game between Brookdale High and a school that was one-hundred percent white. The game was held in our gymnasium one afternoon and the bleachers were packed—integration on our side, all white faces on the other side. I looked across the gym floor and thought: Hey, look at all those white kids over there, the stupid-empty-rich punks! And look at us, in comparison! Our school has three colored kids on the starting team! And our bleachers are *scattered* with black kids—well, not exactly *scattered*, since most of them sat together, but still, man, we were more *progressive* than those blank-faced, backward, lifeless, lily-white punks over there!

And just look at that one colored guy on our team, I thought—look at that kid with the ball, the one who's smiling down there—his name is George Washington and he's president of our Student Council!

Go, Brookdale, go, go, go! Beat the shit out of those All-American boys over there! "Kill 'em!" yelled David Marsh, the All-American boy. So *what* if the black kids were arrogant and cocky at normal times, because we came together through sports! Solidarity and friendship! Go, go, go! And down there at the edge of the basketball court was none other than Joyce Clarkson, a cheerleader! She went to a party in the Flats! And she's yelling and I'm yelling and the black kids are yelling, all together in one big ball of integrated emotion against you uninspiring suburban white kids! Go, Joyce, go!

To be honest, I started getting some pretty bad dreams involving Negroes, probably because Joyce was going through this stage of hers. I dreamt I was swimming at the Bushmont Beach and Yacht Club when suddenly the face of one of my black classmates appeared and said, "Why can't I swim here?" I had a whole lot of that type of dream, and then I started getting some extremely violent ones, most having to do with the Flats, which I had always thought of as a violent place. In my dreams I'd see the black residents like an army rising up in some horrible way to fight against the people up in Bushmont. And then, obeying the movie director in my skull, I'd envision myself sneaking to the edge of the cliff, shouting for the black folks to come on up, and finally *leading* them in their violence.

It was impossible *not* to be aware of the Flats once I started going to school with kids from there. And that was one of the most fundamental differences between me and my parents—black kids were my contemporaries; I was going to school with them, and my parents were not. It may sound like a silly distinction, but it seemed to make all the difference in the world. The number of black friends my parents had was zero. Ella Washington was their maid, while her son was my classmate. My folks lived entirely in a white world. I did, too, except for school. Which meant that I did happen to have a few black friends. None that I ever invited over, really, but I *thought* of them as friends. And I actually lived with the fear that someday, God forbid, one of my black classmates would confront me with certain realities of my world. They wouldn't have to confront me, personally, or even my parents; all they'd have to do was express a general anger at the fact that they lived in a slum and weren't being groomed for college. And when they did, I'd get angry too. When that time came, I would have to agree with them. If George Washington ever stood up in front of the student body in the auditorium and declared that we should march on Bushmont, he would command instant allegiance. I would be among the first to follow him! I didn't think about this very much, but sometimes it crossed my mind. It was as if the potential anger of my black friends, the potential leadership of someone like George, was a silent time bomb in my life; and when it went off, I would become a different person. It was something my parents couldn't know about, because it wasn't in their lives. In one of my dreams a group of black classmates came to my house to burn it down, and I walked outside to *help them light the match*. How could I explain that to my folks, who had given me everything? Well, I didn't have to, because it never happened.

At one point I noticed that Joyce was spending more and, more time with George Washington, which was sort of *a* "first" at Brookdale High, to my knowledge. Integration in the school was one thing, but interracial dating was another story. And I, being a vigorous-but-silent champion of the blending of cultures, was forced to admit that they were perfectly suited to each other. George Washington, King of the Flats, and Joyce Clarkson, Queen of Suburbia!

It was all very harmless, really. Joyce told me that George was planning to become a lawyer some day and maybe go into big-time politics. Her relationship with him, she explained, was one of "mutual respect." In my wildest wet dreams, I imagined the *three* of us hitting the sack together.

Harmless as it was, their relationship soon became the talk of the whole school. You should have seen Joyce—the center of attention, the "proud female" in person. She knew she had entered some kind of danger zone, so she maintained a blank, queenly expression on her face, the chin pointing upward and the lips not quite concealing a smile. She and George went to a big "blast" at Rhonda Strassburger's mansion, and we all stood around watching them dance together. In fact, one time we unconsciously formed a circle and stared at them while they kissed. You'd have thought the entire United States had achieved racial bliss.

11

A Man of Feeling

"Where have you applied, David dear?"

The face of my Aunt Madeline, my father's sister, was diagonally across the living room from where I sat. All other conversation came to a hushed standstill. Where had I applied? Applied for what, oh Mad Aunt Madeline? Now my answer was supposed to float across the room so that everyone would hear it at the same time. Aunt Madeline had planned it that way.

"Notre Dame, Georgetown, and Villanova," I said. "In that order of preference."

It sounded like a list of country clubs to which I had applied for membership. *In that order of preference!* Christ, I hated the sound of my own snobby, conceited voice. The occasion was a "relative party" at our house on Thanksgiving Day in that senior year of high school. I wasn't in the mood to be quite as thankful as you were supposed to be, not even when Old Gramps gave me a doubled allowance check.

"You know where I went to college?" he asked.

"Come on, Gramps," I said, "you didn't go to college."

"I attended the School of Hard Knocks, David."

Haaah! Big joke, Gramps! Don't tell me—you pushed that broom at age fourteen and started your own marmalade company and you did it without a dime or a high-school diploma. You want to go to a *real* college, Gramps? I'll let you take my place, old buddy! You can major in Broom Pushing and minor in

Roughing It, if you can find any such courses.

Boy, was I in the mood to be unthankful. It was almost as bad as Christmas, when my sisters and little brother and I would attack our presents, our "loot" as we called it, with about as much gratefulness as Henry Ford might have had if you gave him a new car.

The plain fact of the matter, of course, was that I shouldn't have been applying to college at all. College was supposed to help you think more clearly and deeply, to be able to apply your intellect and reasoning powers to situations and problems. Now, I didn't want that at all! Guys like me needed something special—a College of Emotion, to borrow an idea from Neil Ulrich. I didn't want to go to school to become "educated" in terms of English or history or mathematics, because I didn't need those things to fill the role that was cut out for me: to make the smooth transition from Typical American Boy to Conventional American Man. I couldn't fail in life if I tried. And everyone at the Thanksgiving party knew it! This was my big test in life: WILL DAVID MARSH GET INTO THE COLLEGE OF HIS CHOICE? The only college that would have appealed to me was one where I'd be forced to go through some kind of hell. Education? No, down with intellect and up with emotion! Set up a College of Blood, Sweat, and Tears and you would have filled it in a day with guys like me. Anything that involved the weeping and gnashing of teeth. Anything that would enable us to laugh and cry and love and hate. That's what we needed, not a four-year period of academic excellence and career training.

So I didn't want to go to college, period. I knew it wouldn't be a school for emotion, no matter which college I chose. I was so apathetic about it that I didn't even put up a fight when my parents requested me to "shoot for a Catholic college." I was hating college of any kind, even before I went, even before I got accepted. I was already looking around for something to get angry at.

Then why had I applied? Well, the truth about growing up in America was that you had to have a bag that you were looking to crawl into, and you had to know what it was and to aim at it, from about the age of seventeen. I mean, guys in their thirties were becoming presidents of big companies, so it stands to reason that they didn't start out at age twenty-five or even at age twenty. Hell, no, they must have known, right in high school, that they were going into the business world, at least into that general bag, and they must have known that they wanted to get to the top. The truth is, too, that you're pretty lucky if you decide early in life that you're going to be a doctor or lawyer or architect or priest or whatever, because then the System is set up for you, and you know just where you're going, you don't have to ask a single question any more like, "Why am I doing this?" or "What am I doing here?" or "What good is this doing me?" Every step of the way is clear-cut, all you have to do, if you know where you're going, is lift your feet, one step at a time, and climb, baby, climb. You're like those horses with the blinders on. The System digs its soft spurs into your soft flesh, cracks its gentle whip, and even holds a damn carrot in front of your nose, and off you go! I envied those guys who said they were becoming physicists and so on, because they knew just exactly what they had to do well in, and there was no possible way for them to get all screwed up or to start in on a whole lot of self-analysis. I envied them, but *secretly* I felt sorry for them. It was as if they were putting straitjackets on themselves, the old blinders, and practically assuring that they'd develop along very narrow lines. "That man," wrote James Baldwin, "who is forced each day to snatch his manhood, his dignity, out of the fire of human cruelty that rages to destroy it, knows if he survives his effort, and even if he does not survive it, something about himself and human life that no school on earth — and indeed, no church — can teach." No school? No church? Then why was I applying to three schools run by the Catholic Church? Two strikes against me!

Meanwhile, the guys who were crawling into definite career bags were at the opposite end of the spectrum from a guy like Eddie Reilly, who was like a balloon floating out of the atmosphere; and that left people like myself, who were in the middle, who wanted to mark time, to rebel against getting tied down too early but not to rebel *too* much, to stay out of the clutches of the System but still to remain in the same room with it, to flirt with it but not to go to bed with it. Thus were created the Liberal Arts schools, the Humanities curriculums, the Great Books programs, the Communication Arts departments, and so on, in greater degree and number than ever before. The appeal was not to those who wanted specific careers, but who wanted some sort of vague, general feeling of having come in contact with the blood of life. The programs enabled you to go to college and get the degree without knowing how to tie a shoelace for a living. You could go right through college and come out knowing not a practical thing. Perfect! Perfect for a whole slice of a generation of cautious rebels, of dreamers. Terrible, though, for guys who wanted to be artists, or dropouts from the System, although they didn't warn you about that. Perfect for kids who would go on to graduate school, or become teachers, or enter social work, but terrible for kids like me, who hadn't a great deal of guts to begin with, because we'd have no guts at all when we were finished. The college diploma was our insurance, something to fall back on, and just knowing you can fall back on something means that you're already beginning to lean on it.

So if I wanted to be a man of feeling, which I did, then it wasn't to my advantage to spend four years getting that insurance. I'd be paying more than time or money for it, I knew that in my bones. To become a man of feeling you had to throw away all the life preservers, cut the anchor rope, bust your compass, and set sail on a whole new life, to become reborn in another place inside another skin. But America won't let you do that, I thought, only to be confronted by the sight of Eddie Reilly coming through the front door, with a little gleam in his eyes.

"What was ND's final record in football this year?" asked my long-legged, gawky cousin Jeffrey as I watched Eddie being greeted by my mother. How do I know what fucking Notre Dame did in fucking football, Cousin Jeffrey?

I ignored his question and gazed at my dear friend, my pal from the Valley Stream Stinkers. Even on Thanksgiving Day he wore a pair of tan khaki pants instead of some dressy slacks. He was sporting a three-inch-wide, light-blue tie with yellow flowers on it, although at the time *thin* ties were in fashion. And though it was winter, Eddie's face had a wonderful, deep tan (where, where in hell—in some private hell he had been born with?—did he get it from?). He spotted me from the hallway and smiled as if to say, "I didn't really want to come, but now that I'm here I might as well have a few laughs."

Okay, Reilly, laugh it up! This was a relative, or family, party. My parents had decided to invite the Reillys because their five grown children were all over the globe and unable to spend Thanksgiving at home. None of the older Reillys were married. Peter was a member of the Secret Service, Barbara was a nurse somewhere in South America, Anne was an airline stewardess who lived in Paris and Hong Kong, Richard was a Jesuit priest teaching in the Midwest somewhere, and Catherine, a social worker living in New York City, was spending Thanksgiving with a room full of orphans. Enough for any parents to boast about, but Dr. and Mrs. Reilly somehow managed to give the impression of total modesty when it came to their children. Mrs. Reilly never seemed to be *aware* that her children were doing such interesting things. On the other hand, my mother took every opportunity to boast of my skimpy achievements. The guests practically had to genuflect in front of my bowling trophies on the mantelpiece.

Anyhow, Eddie came into the living room and sat down on the couch next to me. After him came Mrs. Reilly, a large woman who looked as though she had just come over from a farm in Ireland. She had on the same faded-pink cotton dress that she wore in the summertime, and she, like the dress, seemed to fade into the room and disappear, huge and big-breasted though she was.

Then through the door, making his grand entrance, was the head of the Reilly household, the doctor himself, assisted by little Eileen, who was at this point about thirteen years old. The white-haired general practitioner gripped his daughter's arm firmly, smiled, bowed, and beamed red blushes all over the room. Despite his Parkinson's disease or multiple sclerosis or whatever, there was a man who enjoyed himself! Who squeezed life through a strainer of pain! Eileen held out a firm forearm and eased him into a chair.

Eddie never spoke about his father. It was taken for granted that he admired his old man to the point of worship. But I should explain my admiration for Dr. Reilly. It wasn't just that here was Eddie's old man and therefore I thought a good deal of him. No, it was more basic than that. Dr. Reilly, in my unmedical opinion, was a cripple; and it's a wry reflection on the extent of my imagination, but I thought of cripples as special people. Anyone who suffered inconvenience. Maybe they *are* special people, but I went overboard. After the most superficial observation of cripples, I attributed to them all kinds of profound tragic dimensions. I'd see a guy with one leg, or a blind man, and I'd think, "There goes a tragic hero!" I mean, with Dr. Reilly struggling and smiling his way to the center of attention in my placid household, it made me think how painless life had been for my own father and mother. False, maybe, but such were the thoughts of a son of a typical American family!

Anyway, there we were: Eddie and me on the couch; his modest mother, heroic father, and shy sister; and my depressingly normal family and relatives. Happy Thanksgiving! But you see, we hadn't been called together on this occasion to get down on our knees, no, we were there to *compete,* like the Americans we were, with each other. More specifically, my mother was so proud of me that she wanted to end the argument (what argument, Mom? Has anyone ever disputed you?), once and for all, in her favor: THE JUDGES HAVE CONCLUDED THAT DAVID MARSH IS THE MOST PERFECT BEING CREATED YET IN THIS IMPERFECT WORLD. AMEN!

Mother: "David got a hundred percent in geometry."

Mrs. Reilly: "Oh, that's nice."

Mother: "Thank you. He's a creative person, as well."

Meanwhile, my father was telling Dr. Reilly all about a big deal he had made over martinis the week before. Yes, his agency had snatched a pretzel account from another agency, and so on, you see (visions of my father "swinging the deal" while nearly falling off his bar stool), and out of politeness he asks Dr. Reilly, "Well, how are things going with you?" The tragic hero attempts a reply and I have visions of him crawling up three flights of stairs to get to his poverty-stricken patients. Yes, he worked in the Flats in Brookdale, in a veritable poor section of suburbia. "Oh, fine," was the doctor's reply.

And Uncle Sam (yes, I have an Uncle Sam—why not?), who is Aunt Madeline's husband, suddenly shouted, "For example!" Uncle Sam, you see, was a college professor (still is) for a small girls' college. A pipe smoker, a deep thinker. Fond of locking himself into twenty-minute gazes at the ceiling and suddenly bursting into a vocal communication with no one in particular.

"For example of *what?*" said my father, leaning toward Uncle Sam, whom he despised for being concerned neither with money nor success. No, that was not the proper image for an Uncle Sam. My father had a habit of saying, "Your Uncle Sam, he deliberately wears those tattered brown sports jackets, and he never cuts his hair. He tries to make himself out to be a Daniel Boone of education or something. You know what I think? I think he's just afraid to face life, to compete in the real world."

Perhaps, oh Buffalo Dad. But which of us has a corner on reality?

Anyway, before Uncle Sam could explain his irrelevant

outburst, Mad Aunt Madeline was asking Eddie where *he* had applied to college.

"Harvard," replied Eddie Reilly.

"I beg your pardon?"

Yes, just about everybody in the room was begging Eddie's pardon all at once, because he had succeeded in giving me and Cousin Jeffrey a figurative kick in our educated balls. Of course, he was only kidding about Harvard. "Eddie!" shouted Mrs. Reilly, speaking for the first time (and I have visions of her dragging Eddie across his lawn by one ear). "Tell them the truth, Edward! Don't lie!"

Strong stuff, Mrs. Reilly! Especially compared to my mother's general admonishments. My old lady would have *backed me* up in the lie.

"I really haven't applied to Harvard," said my friend.

"I thought not," said Aunt Madwoman, who smiled in relief. "As a matter of fact, I was under the impression that you weren't going to college at all."

"Then why did you ask me where I had applied?"

"Well, I ..."

Sock it to her, Ed! He had caught my Aunt Malicious with a mouthful of bullshit. Beautiful!

But Aunt Maddening recovered and said, "I am right, however, in assuming that you have renounced higher education?"

"Yeah."

"Oh, that's a shame. I am sorry. You mean to say that you *really and truly* have decided to sidestep a chance at *improving* yourself?"

"Hunh?"

"Eddie, dear, do you mean to say you don't *want* to go to college?"

"That's right."

"Why not, poor darling?"

"Don't wanna."

"Oh, that *is* a pity," said Aunt Madeline, and can you imagine that she was *smiling* throughout this cross-examination?

"I think," said Eddie, "that college makes you lazy."

"What?"

"It's sort of like a country club."

"Country club?"

"Yeah, you know. A little of this, a little of that."

"Come again?"

"Or like a nursery school. Four years of playing on the swings."

Before Aunt Madhatter could assemble her next reply, my grandfather pounded his fist on the coffee table and shouted, "I agree with you, son! A country club! A nursery! Why, when I was fourteen, I was —"

Pushing a broom! God, it seemed as though my grandfather's entire life had been forged from the strokes of that broom, that the experience of pushing debris into a basket had left an indelible mark on his character. On he went, condemning college and the modern age (I think I agreed with him, too) and causing my parents to fidget, since at the moment I was the only human being in the room who happened to be applying to a country club-nursery school. Okay, Gramps, but what's the *point* of it all? See, Gramps and I eventually resolved the issue between us, agreeing that while college was a *terrible* thing, a *waste* of time, and a system producing a mass of non-heroic weaklings, it was necessary to go "in this day and age" in order to compete and succeed. "I agree with you," Gramps had said to me, "that it would be ridiculous for *you* to try to do what I did. You certainly can't go down to Wall Street and ask for a job sweeping the halls." There's the rub! Talk all you want about Abe Lincoln and his logs and his candlelight, but we'll never see such a thing here in the Village of Bushmont. They give us rich white kids all the history about how great our forefathers were, how rugged and individualistic they were, and yet it's *impossible* for us to emulate them! Oh, yes: Buffalo Dad built me a prefabricated log cabin in the backyard when I was eleven, but Eddie Reilly laughed at it, with justification.

Okay, enough! Old Gramps was condemning college. He was on Chapter Four of *Working My Way Up* when my mother spoke up to defend the Modern American Way Of Life in my behalf. But her defense was purely emotional: "Did you all know," she roared, stunning my grandfather into silence, "that David was born with a caul?"

"A *what?*" asked someone in the room.

"A caul. David was born with a blue veil around his head, at birth. It was the rarest thing! My doctor said it was the first time he had seen it. He said it meant that David was destined to become someone special."

Christ, Mom, go all the way, why don't you? Tell them it was a Virgin Birth!

"People used to lean over his baby carriage," she went on, "and remark at what a beautiful child he was."

Yes, and I had heard this story often enough, too. Every Thanksgiving, in fact. Mom! These same relatives have been hearing this same story for years and years! But go on, tell it again! Tell 'em how my first words were an echo of all those leaning, gooing, gurgling, admiring adults. Tell 'em what I said as I looked up at the mirror of myself in the older generation's eyes: "WHAT A BOOT-I-FUL CHILD!"

"And David's first words were—"

Ahhhhhhhhh!

My mother waited for a bit of applause. I did, too. After all, I was conditioned to being patted on the back.

"Only a mother," said my old man, "could jump from broom-pushing to blue veils with such clear logic."

"It's true," said my mother, referring to my first spoken words.

I think that my father was embarrassed by Mom's emotional response. He said, "Was it the doctor who said the caul meant something special, or was it that foolish priest?"

"It might have been the priest, and he wasn't foolish. It could have been Father Leslie. Yes, I think it was. He said it was a sign that David was born into greatness, that he was born under a star."

"Now, now," my father broke in, "the priest didn't actually *tell* you that. You put the words into his mouth. I was there when we had that discussion."

"What, are you *denying* that your own son is someone very special?"

"Of course not," said my father, almost visibly backing into a corner. "Did I say anything against David? I was just—"

"Please!" I shouted. "Will the two of you stop arguing over how goddamn *unique* I am? I'm not unique at all! I've never had any *chance* to be unique. And I don't think I ever will!"

"David!" screamed my mother.

"Listen," I said, "if Eddie doesn't want to go to college, that's his business. *That's* unique, *not* going to college. Anyway, just because I've applied to college doesn't mean I'm any *better* than him. I may not even get accepted, for all I know. Veil or no veil!"

"What are you talking about?" said my old man. "Don't sell yourself short. We never said you were unique. We're not the kind of parents who claim their child is a genius. I'm *glad* you're not a genius, son. But I do say that you're *well-rounded,* hear? And you *believe* in yourself, that's the key to—"

"I thought you weren't going to build me up, Dad!"

"Which would you prefer," said my mother, tears coming into her eyes, "that we *run you down* instead?"

"Yes, as a matter of fact!"

Somewhere along in this dreadful Thanksgiving Day party, the subject of my "interest in acting and theatre" came up. It was Aunt Madeline speaking, at the dinner table. She was being very perceptive: "Your mother tells me that you're going to audition for the winter play at school, David. Do we have another Clark Gable among us?"

"Ha ha."

"It's odd," continued Aunt Madeline, "but America is producing less and less great artists, in every category."

"How would you know?" said Uncle Sam. "After all, it depends on what your definition of art is."

"Well, dear, there are certain *fundamentals.* There are certain general and eternal qualities about great art that never change. And those qualities, those inherent characteristics, cannot be learned in school. It's an old saying that you can't *teach* someone to be a great artist."

Uncle Sam, the teacher, bowed his head in submission to his wife's latest rebuttal. As for myself, I should have kept silent, but I took her comment personally. "Aunt Madeline," I said, "someday I just may become a great actor. I mean, it's possible."

"Well, it's very likely that you could get one of those parts in a television show. One of those soap operas, you know?"

"That wouldn't interest me at all," I said.

"Why not, David?"

Why do adults toy with young people's futures? "Because," I answered, "I'm interested in playing the great roles, like Hamlet."

"Hamlet! Oh, my, my, my. Hamlet! My goodness, David, you could never play Hamlet!"

"Why not?"

"Well, it's obvious, dear."

"It is not! How do you know whether I'm capable of becoming a great actor or not?"

"David, dear, I know that to be a great artist, one must have suffered. One must have had experience in grief. And I know that you, my dear, thanks to your wonderful parents, have never had to really feel pain."

"Oh, yes I have," I lied.

"Come now, David, you have always been a happy boy."

"*Is that a crime?*" asked my mother, pleading for assistance out of her confusion.

She received no help from me.

<h1 style="text-align:center">12</h1>

On the Stage

Soon after that I tried out for the high-school play. They were doing *Arsenic and Old Lace*, the farce-comedy about two crafty but mentally unbalanced old ladies who poison lonely old men to put them out of their misery. For some time I had been planning to audition for the big school production no matter what the play was, but I did harbor a preference for serious drama. I would have selected something a bit longer on emotion and shorter on slapstick. I wasn't anti-laughter or anything, but I was thinking more along the lines of *Death of a Salesman* or *The Glass Menagerie*. But a play is a play.

"It sounds like a stupid play, all right," commented Edward Reilly, the Supreme Valley Stream Stinker.

"Listen, Ed, I have to start someplace, you know. It's the only play they're doing, so I'm gonna try out for it, do you mind? I've been thinking about being an actor for more than a year now."

Ah, but my voice lacked conviction. Looking back, I can see that I was born, raised and thoroughly conditioned as an Establishment person. If *Arsenic and Old Lace* was all that the System offered, I joined it with a shrug of complacency and acceptance. If they were auditioning for *Kiss My Ass, Nigger*, undoubtedly I would have tried out for it. Anything to succeed!

"If I were you," said Eddie, "I'd make up my *own* play and put it on."

"But nobody would come and watch it."

"So what?"

Arsenic and Old Lace, I found out, had been a big success back around 1941, when I was born. No experimental theatre for the Class of '59, that was sure.

I went to the tryouts with Kenny Starro, who shared my interest in the theatre to the extent that he wanted to be a professional dancer someday. "I need your support," I told him as we walked into the auditorium after school. I looked nervously around at the competition. I had read the play and was going to try for the part of Mortimer. Miss Munch, our 200-pound drama coach, had prepared typewritten lists of the characters. Mortimer was described as a "lively, amiable, politely fresh young man, of no particular type." Archie Andrews! Perfect!

About three-fourths of the kids in the auditorium were girls. Of the eight or nine boys, two were black, and believe it or not I was thinking, "Well, we can eliminate those two, because there just aren't any black characters in the play! How 'bout *that,* man? And that ain't discrimination, neither—it's *fact.*" That's what I was thinking, being so hungry for the lead role. And most of the other guys, by comparison, just weren't as All-American as me. Yes, I was secure and confident as hell. See, the athletes hardly ever tried out for the plays, and in fact most of the male thespians, like Kenny Starro, were looked upon as sort of "faggoty". There were a couple of real fat guys and one pint-sized kid. Most of the guys trying out were so-called eggheads, and physically out of shape. All of which made me terrifically happy, because here was a contest I was going to win hands-down. Here was Competition at its bloodthirsty best, the greed salivating from the walls of my gut; and all I had to do was stand on the stage and show Miss Munch my normal body, white skin, blue eyes, innocent face, and average speech pattern.

"Miss Munch! Miss Munch!"

That was me, yelling like an idiot, running into her office to "express my gratitude" for her having cast me in the role of Mortimer.

"This means so much to me," I said. "I can't thank you enough. But tell me, did I get the part because of my audition? I mean, was it because of how well I read the lines? Or because I just *looked* right?"

"Do you want to know the truth?"

"Sure, Miss Munch."

"Well, David, let's just say you were type-cast."

"But I thought that Mortimer was 'of no particular type.' "

"Exactly."

"Didn't my audition count for *anything?*"

"Oh, of course it did. Your audition proved that you can walk and talk."

"Is that all?"

"Perhaps you have potential. But to be very honest, I did *not* cast you in the role on the basis of your acting ability."

Angry, I mumbled, "Then why didn't someone else get the part?"

"There were some very talented students auditioning, extremely talented boys. But they just didn't fit the part as well as you did. I had to make a choice between ability and suitability, ha ha."

"Thanks," I said with not a little sarcasm.

"Look at it this way, David. If you're interested in acting, you'll undoubtedly succeed sooner than other people, because you're a type that's in demand. There's a big market for your 'product,' so to speak."

"That sounds like a backhanded compliment, Miss

Munch."

"It is, in a sense. I'm telling you that before you do anything, before you learn to act on stage, you have a distinct advantage. You're clean-cut, although you could stand a haircut, and you have no outstanding features, one way or another."

Try me, Miss Munch! I'll show you an outstanding feature you won't soon forget! Right between those cannon-legs of yours!

"What I mean to say, David, is that you're a perfect 'boy-next-door' type, which should give you a lot of confidence in yourself."

I should point out that Miss Munch was round and pink and prematurely gray, a typical Mother Hen with little high-school girls for her flock. She was constantly listening to the girls' problems and agreeing with them about how their parents didn't understand them. She loved the girls, loved how they ran to her, how they sobbed in her lap after school—and also told her of their hostility toward the male species. Miss Munch called them her girls—"*My girls* are the most important people in my life." She was sort of their second mother and all that crap, while with the boys she was strictly honest, at times to the point of outright mockery.

"Miss Munch," I broke in, "it doesn't really give me any confidence to be thought of as the boy next door. In fact, it depresses me."

"Oh, poor little boy. It 'depresses' you, eh? Yet you'll grow up and marry the *girl* next door and turn her into a domestic slave, won't you? No, David, you shouldn't be depressed. You couldn't fail in life if you tried. I mean, you *could* fail, but only if you got run over by a truck. That's the truth, and your audition only reinforced it."

"I don't follow you, Miss Munch."

"You don't have to follow me. Just show up at

rehearsals on time and be prepared to learn your lines and blocking. I'll expect you to be as dedicated to the group effort as you are capable of being."

"Miss Munch," I said, trembling at her tone, "what gives you the idea that I won't be dedicated, or that I won't join a group effort?"

"Did I say that?"

"No, but you implied —"

"I implied, correctly, that you, David, have been geared to a selfish way of life, as opposed to a team spirit."

"Look," I said, not knowing what the hell I was talking about, "I'm a liberal."

Miss Munch really got a laugh over that one. "David," she said, "you're very charming. You're like an Army or Navy man on leave in a foreign country — unaware of your basic egotism, but still charming."

The nerve of this woman! First she casts me in the goddamn lead role of the play, and then she seems *angry* at having to accept me! If I caught the vibrations correctly, Miss Munch hated my guts. For the first couple of weeks of rehearsals I kept trying to figure out what it was about me that she so despised. Failing to see what anybody in the world could have against me, I went on the defensive. I imagined that to Miss Munch I was a symbol of male superiority, and in my daydreams I conceived of her as a secret revolutionary guerrilla in some sort of feminist movement. Ah, that would explain why Miss Estelle Munch — my discoverer! my stage mother! — seemed to look upon me with such coldness and bitterness and disgust. I actually disgusted her! Me, her prodigy! In the process of putting together this play production, Mis Munch was secretly mobilizing a cadre of female freedom fighters, and no wonder she had chosen *Arsenic and Old Lace,* whose original title was *Bodies In Our Cellar!*

Male bodies, that is.

The play was scheduled to be performed on a Saturday night in January. All the seats had been sold. My parents had purchased two rows worth of tickets, near the front of the auditorium. Our Friday-night dress rehearsal had gone badly. At one point Miss Munch angrily accused me of looking like a male version of Miss America. "You're too *charming*," she yelled.

On Saturday afternoon I was nervous as hell. I walked around my living room, going over the scenes in my head, and couldn't even remember my lines! God, I had studied them backward and forward, but now my mind was absolutely blank. The prospect of standing out there in front of six hundred people, without a thought in my head, frozen in brain and body, filled me with a kind of terror that rendered me so weak that I thought I'd have to climb into bed and never get up again.

"What have I gotten myself into?" I cried out loud.

To make matters worse, Eddie Reilly stopped over at the house to inform me that he was planning to attend the play.

"Are you really gonna come, Ed?"

"Yep."

"I thought you didn't like plays."

"I don't, but I figured it was good for some laughs."

"Thanks a lot, buddy."

"Besides, your mother sent me a free ticket."

"She did?"

"Yeah. She said it was right in the third row, in the middle."

I don't know where all my blood ran to in that moment, but it felt as though I had none left inside me.

I started pacing around the living room like an animal. "Listen," I said too loudly, "you'd better not mess me up, Reilly. If you start giggling or something, I'll—"

"Why not? I thought it was supposed to be a *comedy*."

"*It* is, but—"

"Then I *should* have a few chuckles at it, right?"

"Sure, Ed, sure. Just don't laugh in the wrong places, that's all. If you find yourself going out of control or anything, just excuse yourself and go to the men's room, okay?"

In fact, I thought, why don't you go there right in the beginning? After Eddie left I took a shower and did some pushups in my room, naked.

I didn't even go downstairs for dinner. Why in hell had I gotten myself into this thing? I figured that I should have made a rule, right in the beginning of my acting career, that I'd only do tragedy and never a comedy. I thought it would be easier to "get into a role" if it had some "meat" in it. I mean, I hadn't thought about being an actor in order to get up on stage and be funny—just the opposite! Suddenly I couldn't even imagine myself on that stage, in a few hours, walking around as Mortimer. I had never even figured out who Mortimer *was,* much less remembered the lines. Miss Munch had done nothing in the way of helping me work out an "inner life" for the character. In a panic I started reading *An Actor Prepares* for the umpteenth time, hoping to find some clue to finding a sense of purpose in the whole thing. "Our aim is not only to create the life of a human spirit, but also to express it in a beautiful, artistic form." What? For Mortimer in *Arsenic and Old Lace?* Mortimer had no human spirit at all, at least none that I had created.

Before curtain time for a high-school play, everybody keeps you so busy doing one thing or another that you never get a chance to collect your thoughts. Some makeup girl grabbed me and threw me into a chair and started sponging up my face and putting on eye shadow and crap. This was *her* big artistic moment, and she wasn't about to let me deprive her of it. For thirty minutes she worked on my face like it was the goddamn Mona Lisa, yet when I opened my eyes I looked in the mirror and saw The Boy Who Owns Lassie! All that makeup, all that fussing over my facial features, and I came out looking like a kid on the way to his first suburban paper route. I suddenly began to envy the guys who played "character" parts, because their makeup really obscured their bland appearances.

In the Green Room, Miss Munch gave us a pep talk: "I want to say that I regard you all as my very own children. We've come a long way from the auditions and the first reading of our script. Tonight, we go out there in full costume, in a beautifully designed set, to breathe life into what once were merely words on the printed page. We are on the last mile of a long journey. You are all my children, and tonight I shall be sitting in the audience, watching you blossom to full maturity in a span of less than three hours. My work is done. My labor pains are over. Now it's your show. I love you all, as a mother —"

And Miss Munch began to cry! Unbelievably, crazily, the woman started wiping the mascara from beneath her eyes. Three of the girls in the play walked up and put their arms around her. They gave her a pink corsage to wear on her light-gray dress, and the woman literally wept. As we filed out of the Green Room to the corridor, and then to the stage door, she kissed each of us. When it was my turn she hugged me and said, "Go out there, David, and whatever you do, *enunciate.*" I told her I would do that, if I could remember any of my lines. "You will, dear," she said. "You will, because now you're one of my babies."

The curtain went up and I waited, with paralytic fear, to make my entrance. At last the moment came and I stepped into the lights. Surprisingly, I remembered my lines! I was acting! But I had no control over myself. The words were coming out as if from a machine separate from my body. The audience chuckled. Then they began to laugh out loud at the situations of the play, and I reacted to the laughter with violent physical gestures. Up went my eyebrows, out went the arms, and soon my voice was rising up the scale. It rose at least two octaves and turned into an English accent! I had never known that I *had* one. My ancestors hadn't been Anglo-Saxons for nothing! Under the spotlight, my true colors emerged!

Out on that stage, I felt as though my mind were somewhere inside a goldfish bowl of jelly, and my body felt like the bottom half of a worm, wriggling from shock and the unleashing of excessive tension. I no longer listened to the other actors, couldn't even *see* them, and my ears and eyes could only make out a steady blur of sound-image. I could hear my *own* voice, speaking Mortimer's lines with the goddamn English accent, and I could hear the audience laughing. Was I *that* funny?

At the first intermission I rushed through the corridor and into the boys' dressing room. What had I done? I supposed that I had just delivered the most phenomenal first-act performance ever, or else I had made a rather large ass of myself. I looked in the mirror and could see Miss Munch walking through the door behind me. As she approached, her massive body, usually so erect on its delicate frame, was slumping down like a warm mound of gray ice cream; and her cheeks – normally propped up, somehow, over the square jawbone – were now sagging in all directions. Oh Miss Munch, how I paint thee in unflattering colors!

As I turned to face her, she waddled over beside me and crashed, out of breath, into a fold-up chair. She straddled it backwards, her thighs again looking like two cannons spread to the corners of the room.

"David," she whispered as though she had just crossed a desert and climbed a peak to reach me, "where did you get the British accent, dear?"

"My father's side of the family," I said.

"David, dear, you must *control* your performance. You're using too much energy, like modern art. David …"

Modern art! I took it as a compliment. I waited for her to finish, but she was looking at me from the face of a pig about to be slaughtered. Had I been *that* bad?

"More control, David."

"Control?"

"Yes. Please … please control your gestures, your speech. Don't—"

"Don't what?"

"Don't …"

Miss Munch was speechless and breathless. A flood of sweat permeated the material of her gray dress.

Then the second act got under way, and this time I went out there and "controlled" the hell out of everything. Trying to avoid exaggeration in my performance, I went in the other direction and mumbled through the whole act. It is the fate of the Empty American, I suppose, to either overact or underact, for lack of any substance. The result of my underplaying was an enormous silence on the part of the audience. Naturally I took this as an intense interest in my acting. Not so. During the next intermission Miss Munch, now a floating mass of perspiration, informed me that it was nothing more nor less than boredom.

"Oh, David," she cried, "go back to the way you did it in the first act. Excess energy is better than nothing at all. Please, David, put some *life* into it."

In the third act, I alternated between one extreme and the other. First I'd shout one line, then mumble the next. Back and forth between mania and limpness. There seemed to be no middle ground. I possessed no center of gravity. The only line I did well was, "Elaine! Did you hear — do you understand? — I'm a bastard!"

"The trouble with your performance," said the Mad Philosopher, "was that you didn't telegraph any basic gurgitations from the psychic core of your bowels to the intellectual elevators in your memory."

"Would you please rephrase that?"

"Why don't you *listen* to me!" Neil demanded, breathing heavily and wiping the saliva from his chin.

"Well, tell me again, dammit. You're over my head."

"When you get on a stage," he said, "think of it as an outhouse. All the world's an outhouse. When you say a line, think of how you feel when you're taking a shit. It's a moment of pure truth."

The other Valley Stream Stinkers were not much more help. Eddie, of course, thought that the whole thing was hilarious, but he wasn't referring to the play. What made Eddie laugh was the simple fact that here were a bunch of students being phony.

"But Eddie, the word 'phony' isn't exactly accurate. I mean, it's a *deliberate* illusion. It's the *nature* of a play that it's phony. What your trouble is, Ed, is that you can't suspend your disbelief."

"Hunh?"

"You couldn't get it out of your mind that it was *me* up there on stage, Ed. If you'd been able to suspend your disbelief, you would've forgotten all about me."

"But it *was* you up there," Eddie replied with a broad smile.

This conversation was typical of many I'd had with Eddie Reilly over the years, and it occurred to me that I'd never make a good President of the United States, because Eddie and I would *still* be having the same conversation. I could just imagine myself giving the inaugural address and suddenly hearing Eddie's high-pitched laughter rise from the crowd.

And of course Kenny Starro was just the opposite from Eddie. He was ready to believe *any* illusion, especially when it was part of the theatre. "David," he said, "you were simply grand! I cried. I really did. I just *bawled.*"

"What'd you do that for, Kenny? I mean, the goddamn play was a *comedy.*"

"I couldn't help it. When the curtain went down and everybody applauded and you took your bows, I just couldn't hold it back. It was a great moment in the theatre."

Anything in the theatre, to Ken Starro, was a great moment. In the course of a school year, he went down to Broadway to see shows at least thirty times. And he must have seen *The Wizard of Oz* a hundred different times. Yes, Kenny was hooked on Judy Garland. He could imitate the way she planted her feet on stage in order to belt out a song, and the walls of his room were plastered with her pictures. Just *talking* about Judy Garland made him cry on the spot. Frankly, I envied him a great deal.

13

Hamlet and Me

In early February of senior year our English class was studying *Hamlet,* and it suddenly occurred to me that it was very depressing to be sitting there in a boring classroom studying all about a tragic hero who might have been my own age. So I took my book home one day, got in bed, and discovered that aside from getting up to go to the bathroom, I was unable to leave my bed at all. I'd rush out to the toilet, then scramble back under the covers.

My parents came upstairs to plead with me. They begged my forgiveness. "You're forgiven," I told them. "But it has nothing to do with you two. I just can't get up, that's all. I'm not motivated. The circumstances of my life at this given moment simply do not compel me into any specific action."

"It's the goddamn acting," said my father. "Stop talking like a goddamn actor."

"Life *is* action," I replied. "Action produces friction. Friction causes emotion. I am dead."

"Is there something we can do?" asked my mother. "How have we failed you?"

"You haven't failed me. I love you both. There's nothing anyone can do. I'll have to do it myself, but I don't know what . . ."

"We want to *communicate* with you, David," said the old man.

"What's on your mind, Dad?"

"What's on *your* mind, son?"

"Nothing. Absolutely nothing."

"Do you hate us?" my mother asked.

"Of course not. I've always had everything I've wanted. I can't remember a time when I was punished unjustly. I just don't want to get up."

"Maybe the two of us should get away together for a few days," my father suggested. "We could rent a little place out on the tip of Long Island and maybe go fishing. Just you and me, Dave. The two of us, like we used to. We'll *rough* it. Whaddya say, Dave?"

"I'll think about that, Dad. I really will."

A week went by, and my mother brought up a portable television set, but eventually I pulled out the plug. Then I refused all meals. I became too weak to masturbate. Besides, the sheets were getting stiff. I curled up in a fetal position, with my thumb in my mouth, and dreamt of James Dean, of my grandfather pushing his broom, of Dr. Reilly crawling up to his patients in the slums, of Mr. Greene the Jew, of my father shooting Nazis, of Jesus Christ and the Brooklyn Dodgers, of George Washington the Negro and of Stanislavski. And sometimes I sat up straight, in the middle of the night, my heart pounding at the thought that Eddie was still waiting for me at the bridge.

At this point I'm afraid we go from bad to worse. I was supposed to be going to school, but it gave me a good deal of pleasure to think that I was disturbing the rigid structure of my life. While in bed, I began to immerse myself in *Hamlet*, reading each scene carefully and reciting the lead character's lines aloud. The effect was marvelous; it transported me into a new existence. Somehow I figured that if I could *become* Hamlet, in some sense at least, I might be able to achieve those qualities of personality and character which I knew neither Brookdale High nor any other school could teach me. I utilized a small paperback edition until its pages began to fall out, requiring me to tape them back to the binding. Soon I rose from my bed and walked around the house like an apparition. I did so while pondering and then speaking Hamlet's soliloquies. I recited aloud, from memory, the famous "To be or not to be" speech at least twenty times while sitting on the stair landing, elbow on knee and chin on fist. In the backyard I recited to the sky, again from memory, the "Too, too solid flesh" speech. From the soliloquies I progressed to a scene-by-scene memorization of Hamlet's words, never speaking directly to my parents. My hair had grown pretty long, and I wore only black shirts and pants, with white sneakers. And I actually managed to grow a slight beard.

Eventually I learned to respond to my family using only lines from *Hamlet*. For about three weeks my folks, not wishing to unleash full-scale rebellion or latent violence in their mad son, attempted to play along with the gag. Not that they went out and bought copies of *Hamlet* in order to communicate with me; they merely attempted to exhibit complete unawareness that our relationship had, to say the least, become a bit strained.

I'd hear my parents discussing something downstairs and I'd yell, *"Wormwood! Wormwood!"*

No answer, but imagine the expressions on their faces as they stared at each other down in the living room.

"Oh, my prophetic soul! Mine uncle!"

I imagined my father taking a drink while Mom stood listening for additional outbursts from her parrot of a son upstairs.

"These tedious old fools!"

And then, after a strategy meeting over two martinis apiece, they'd march upstairs to confront me.

"Hillo, ho, ho, boy! Come, bird, come!"

I'd be sitting on my bed as they trooped into the room. *"Then came each actor on his ass."*

The two of them would peek through the door and then come in as though they were entering a psychiatric ward. "David," said my father on one occasion, "we'd like to speak with you."

"Speak, sir, a whole history."

"Please, David," my mother said. "Your father—"

"Ay, what of him?"

"You're making us both quite upset," cried the old man.

"With drink, sir?"

"I'm going to have a nervous breakdown!" shouted my mother.

"Oh, wonderful son, that can so astonish a mother!"

"You be respectful of your mother!"

"We shall obey, were she ten times our mother."

"David," said the old man in a more reasonable tone, "you've got to snap out of this. You're missing school, and we can't cover up for you forever. Besides, you have such a good mind, and—"

"So I do still, by these prickers and stealers."

Indeed, Mom and Dad, I thought, what are you worried about? I have friends who've *beat up* their parents when they didn't like something. I know a kid who ran away from home to become a gigolo! There are friends of mine who've gotten screwed up on alcohol and drugs, who've had illegitimate children, and so on! I know one guy who set fire to his parents' summer cottage because he didn't like material goods! And forty-nine girls who have cut their wrists in bathrooms all over Bushmont! So what are you worried about if *your* child wants to play Hamlet for a while!

"David, what's *wrong* with you?"

"*Sir,*" I lied, smiling at the irony, "*I lack advancement.*"

"You lack advancement? Aren't I going to send you to Notre Dame? You can advance to the heights of this *earth* if you want!"

And get into heaven, too, I thought. Man, I've got *everything* going for me.

"You can even be President someday," my mother interjected timidly.

Right! That too, Mom!

"Please, Davey boy, tell us why you continue this way. Is it our fault? We've always been ready to accept the blame, but—"

"*You would play upon me! You would pluck out the heart of my mystery!*"

A few days after this abortive confrontation, I was downstairs in the kitchen when my mother asked me to take out the garbage.

"*I shall in all my best obey you, madam.*"

"While you're out there, why don't you get a little sun? You're awfully pale, dear."

"*The air bites shrewdly, Mother. It is very cold.*"

"I know, but staying inside all the time isn't very good for your health."

"*I do not set my life at a pin's fee.*"

"Would you like to pick up your father at the station?"

"*A little more than kin, and less than kind.*"

I came back from my garbage chore—imagine, Hamlet having to take out the garbage!—and my mother said, "David, guess who I saw in town."

"*For God's love, let me hear!*"

"Joyce Clarkson."

"*Is't possible?*"

"She's—"

"*Speak, I am bound to hear.*"

"She seems to have changed somewhat. How long has it been since you've seen her?"

"A little month. Ere those shoes were old with which she followed my poor father's body, like Niobe, all tears . . ."

"David, please! I spoke to Joyce, and she said she misses seeing you at school."

"Frailty, thy name is woman!" I shouted, stomping into the living room.

My mother followed and seated herself on the arm of the couch, next to me. She began stroking my long hair. "Oh, David, why can't we stop all this?"

"Go, go, you question with a wicked tongue."

"Oh, David—"

"What's the matter now?"

She began to cry. "David, please … I'm your mother, and—"

"No, by the rod! Not so! You are the queen, and, would it were not so, you are my mother."

At moments like this I started hating myself, but there seemed to be no way out of it, at the time. Whatever was the matter with me, I instinctively knew that it wasn't in the power of my mother and father to change it. See, I could have stopped the whole game instantly, if I had wanted to. But for what reason? I was having fun! I *liked* being Hamlet. In fact, as far as I was concerned, Hamlet was a real, live person who actually had lived in history. I could picture him in my mind, very clearly. What I liked best was when he fooled around and antagonized people. Which, I think, was why I enjoyed my own antics so much. For example, where he catches the conscience of the king and so on. That was a great idea. See, I didn't mention this, but I'd had an idea like that myself. I really did. For several months or so I had carried around the idea of producing this mammoth play on a hillside somewhere. The entire world would come see it and I'd catch everybody's conscience:

"I have heard that guilty creatures, sitting at a play, have by the very cunning of the scene been struck so to the soul that presently they have proclaimed their malefactions."

Anyhow, each night the old man would come home for dinner, unload his briefcase, and sit down on the couch for a drink. I suppose he had made up his mind to ignore me. One night I was coming downstairs and my mother said, "David, where's your father?"

Actually he was sitting on the couch, but I replied, with Hamlet's words, *"At supper!"*

"Supper?"

"I am not!" came the old man's voice from the living room.

"Not where he eats, but where he is eaten. A certain convocation of politic worms are eating at him."

Hearing this, the old man charged through the hall to the stair landing. "Goddamn it!" he roared. "I'll have no more of this!"

"Good evening, sir. But what, in faith, make you from Wittenberg?"

Holding his fists down at his sides, he turned to avoid facing his bearded, black-clad, demented offspring.

"The time is out of joint," I said.

"I'm gonna put *you* out of joint," retorted the old man.

"Oh, God, I could be bounded in a nutshell, and—"

"A nut*house!*" shouted my father. "Nut*house!*"

By March my parents had just about given up on me. At night I'd hear them discussing the possible methods of "curing" me. Then one day the phone rang and my mother called upstairs, "David, it's Joyce! She wants to speak with you!"

"No, good mother! Here's metal more attractive!"

"David, why not come down and talk to Joyce, your old friend?"

"Let her not walk in the sun!"

I tiptoed halfway down the stairs and listened to the last part of my mother's conversation with Joyce. "... No, he can't come to the phone ... No, dear, I don't think he *will* call you back ... Joyce, we're having a terrible problem with him ... Well, it's hard for me to explain. He hasn't gone out of the house for more than a month ... I *know* he's missing school ... No, he's not sick, but we still can't get him out of the house, or to speak with anyone on the phone. He won't see any of his friends, not even Eddie, or talk to them. He won't even talk to us, his parents, aside from, well ... Well, Joyce, he speaks only lines from *Hamlet.* I've looked in every kind of book, but ... Oh, no, Joyce, I don't think—well, if you'd like to come over, you're certainly welcome to. In fact, it might do him some good to see you. Maybe you could even *cure* him, ha-ha ... Tomorrow at noon? ... Fine, Joyce. Wonderful. See you then. Thank you, dear."

I was both excited and irritated that Joyce Clarkson was coming over to see me. Mainly I felt an extreme amount of shame, or at least of embarrassment. It had been four or five months since our breakup and yet I hadn't, by any standard, become a man of feeling. And by now Joyce was probably the leader of some gang in the Flats! All kinds of things went through my mind. God, she was living a more full life than I was! And what would she find? A spoiled little kid, dressed up as Hamlet, reciting Shakespeare in bed!

Thoughts of my impending humiliation, and anger at my mother for even *allowing* such a confrontation to take place, should have snapped me out of the Hamlet bag. I either should have gone downstairs and yelled at my mother, saying that I definitely would not see Joyce when she arrived, or I should have transformed myself back into a very happy, college-bound son of Bushmont; or perhaps I should have done both. At least, those would have been my normal reactions.

Instead, I began to shrink away from the prospect of facing Joyce, and to concentrate harder on Shakespeare's world. I sat on my bed and went over Hamlet's lines for hours on end, posing in my long, Christ-like hair, and my beard, and my black shirt and pants — receding from reality as if viewing it from the rear of a speeding train. I kept repeating, *"How weary, stale, flat, and unprofitable seem to me all the uses of this world."*

I was still on my bed when the doorbell rang on that Sunday afternoon. I could hear my father and mother whispering to her, filling her in. And then I heard Joyce coming upstairs.

She came into the room and sat on the edge of my bed, my rumpled prince's berth, and brushed her hair from an eye. She whispered, "Hi, David."

"Is it a free visitation?"

"Sure."

"I know the good king and queen have sent for you."

"Your parents?"

"I see a cherub that sees them."

"Why would they send for me?"

"That, my dear, you must teach me."

She gazed into my eyes with a kind of compassion I hadn't seen since James Dean had looked down at the dead body of Sal Mineo. For the first time in my life, a girl was looking past me into my soul!

"David," she said softly, "what's the trouble?"

"I have of late, but wherefore I know not, lost all my mirth."

She laughed a little and said, "Would you like to take a walk?"

"Into my grave?"

"You're really hung-up, aren't you?"

"I am but mad north-north-west. When the wind is southerly, I know a hawk from a handsaw."

Joyce was being gentle and patient with me, almost as if she were my mother. Trying to change the subject, whatever the subject was, she said, "I'm not dating George anymore."

"Oh, villainy!"

"But I have *changed* a great deal, David. I've learned a great deal from George. He's probably the finest human being I know. Really, David, he is. I'm thinking of majoring in social science in college. And I wanted to tell you, I don't want to live in a house in Bushmont anymore."

"Bushmont's a prison."

"I know."

"A goodly one, in which there are many confines, wards, and dungeons, Bushmont being one of the worst."

Now old Joycie changed her course. She lay down on the bed beside me, putting an arm around my waist. "David," she said, "I'll never forget the way I felt about you. We still have something very special."

"Very like, very like."

"Kiss me?"

"Man delights me not," I said. *"No, nor woman neither."*

"How about just plain me?"

The thing was, I had fallen in love with the girl all over again, but I was too damn embarrassed and angry at myself.

"I still love you," she said.

Suddenly I shot out of bed and stood on a chair. *"Ha, ha!"* I shouted. *"Are you honest?"*

"What?"

"*Are you fair?*"

"I..."

"*If you be honest and fair, your honesty should admit no discourse to your beauty!*"

"Look, David, I didn't come here to be made a fool of."

"*I did love you once!*"

"I know."

"*You should not have believed me.*"

"Okay," she said, shrugging her shoulders.

"*Get thee to a nunnery!*"

She walked slowly from the bedroom. At the door, she turned and said, "We won the basketball game yesterday. The semi-playoff."

"*I have heard of your paintings, too, well enough!*"

I was unable to break out of Hamlet's lines. For once, however, I *wanted* to get back into David Marsh, to stop her from going, but I think I was too afraid of my old self. I couldn't stop treating her like Ophelia.

As she went down the stairs I leaned over the railing and shouted, "*God has given you one face and you make yourself another! You jig, you amble, and you lisp! Go to, I'll no more on it! It hath made me mad!*"

"See you," she called from the front door. "Come back to school soon!"

"*Your loves, as mine to you! Farewell!*"

14

Joyce and Me

Almost as soon as Joyce left I began shedding my Hamlet speech and, along with it, the black clothing. I kept the long hair but shaved off the beard, and I put on some jeans and an old faded brown corduroy shirt. I put on the radio, turning to my favorite "Negro" station, and hummed along as I made the transformation back to normal. My parents were amazed when I came down to dinner and said, "Hi, Mom. Hi, Dad, old pal. What's new on the stock market?"

At dinner they kept waiting for me to suffer a relapse. Occasionally I *did* forget myself and came out with things like, "Thrift, thrift!" and "Angels and ministers of grace!" and "Pr'ythee, say on!" Each time I lapsed into such phrases, bales of phony, horrified laughter were emitted from the openings of my parents' pounding skulls.

I called Joyce that same night. When I apologized for my behavior she said, "Oh, don't be sorry! When I told some of the kids about you, they couldn't *believe* it."

"They couldn't?"

"Oh, they cracked up!"

"They did? Why?"

"Because it's such a nutty, beautiful thing."

"What is?"

"Going around like Hamlet! David, I didn't realize you had such a sense of humor."

Neither did I, Joyce!

"Well," I said, "I'm all finished with that."

"It was outstanding, David. Just outstanding!"

On that cheerful note, I asked her if she'd like to go out "for a few beers, just for old times' sake." The only place we could get served with liquor, being under eighteen, was the Duck Inn, so I mentioned that we could go there. I got out my old secondhand car, the "short," and sped over to her up the street. When she met me at the door the first thing she wanted to know was what happened to the beard. Well, you win some and lose some. We went to the Duck Inn and sat in a corner booth with a pitcher of beer and two glasses.

"Joyce," I said, "you look really great."

"My whole *outlook on life* has changed, David."

"In what way?"

She smoothed down her long blond hair absent-mindedly and thought a moment. "Well, you know that as a little girl I always hated rules. Silly rules."

"Yeah."

"Well, it's that simple. I've finally discovered that if I don't have freedom, I stop being alive. I've been through hell in my seventeen years."

"You have?"

"Certainly. Do I look happy to you?"

"Well, yes and no."

"The answer is no, David. I'm much happier than I was *before* I changed my outlook, but I'm still not *totally* happy."

"I see."

"Last week, I almost threw myself under the wheels of a moving car."

"You did?"

"I almost did, but I didn't. Things had gotten that bad."

"What things?"

"Everything. Anyway, I finally changed my outlook, and I've decided to live my own life, in my own way. I'm finally discovering who I *am*, David."

"Good, good," I said, trying to show a little more enthusiasm than I actually had.

The conversation went along for nearly five hours. We closed up the Duck Inn and Joyce was still jabbering away about rules and freedom. At this point, all I could think of was her body. The more philosophic and "serious" she became, the more I thought of sex. I couldn't even stand up, my hardness was so hard.

On the way home, she outlined a theory of hers that children and young people should get together and vote to disregard all rules made by society, if they feel such rules don't make any sense. "Right from the start," she said, "kids are taught to assume that certain things are absolutely necessary."

"Like what?"

"Well, like eating three meals a day. Who *says* you should eat three meals a day? Why not two, or just one? And like wearing clothes. You just accept it from the moment you're born. But maybe clothes are wrong! Maybe we should all be naked! And take the daytime and nighttime."

"Daytime and nighttime?"

"Sure. When you're a kid, adults tell you that you should go to bed at night and get up in the morning. Because that's what *they* do. But maybe it should be the other way around! Why not sleep in the daytime and do your living at night? How will we ever know what's best if we don't try it? And of course you can extend this to everything, like going to school, and like getting married. Everything! I think each generation should get together and try to start all over again, with a new way of doing things."

Oh, how Joyce Clarkson had changed. It was hard to believe that this was the same girl with whom I had foxtrotted in the ballroom of the Biltmore Hotel in New York City, at her coming-out party. With whom I had parked at the end of so many lonely roads on so many nights!

"I gather, Joyce, that you no longer care much for 'security' and all that."

"Of course I don't. I *loathe* security now. When we had that argument, when we broke up, I was still accepting all the ridiculous rules and behaving like my mother. I believed things about life without questioning them. Now, I'm concerned with the *quality* of things. And with the quality of *people,* too."

"Of people?"

"Sure. I don't judge people in the same way anymore."

"How do you judge them now?"

"By, well, by their *vibrations.* By the amount of sensitivity they seem to have. I can't explain it, really. But you can tell, if you meet someone, whether that person is alive or dead inside. Do you know what I mean?"

Do I know what you mean! Joyce, I thought to myself, what do you think I've been groping after for most of my idiotic life? We had parked outside her house in the dark, and I was waiting for her to say, "And David, you are one of those people who have such a quality." Joyce, can't you see that I was way ahead of my time? Remember all the things I had said about Jimmy Dean? But you had *mocked* me!

With all the quality I could muster, I leaned over and kissed Joyce. All that talk about vibrations and sensitivity had temporarily turned me into a sex maniac. But naturally I didn't go about things in a rough manner or anything; no, I was too romantic for that. I kissed her eyelids and rubbed her thigh and so forth. She responded well, and before long I had undone her bra and was feeling her up pretty good. Ah, nothing had really changed! The usual pattern was emerging: I feel her up while we kiss, and then she unzips my fly; and then, she spits on her hand and quietly jerks me into another world. And now, with all of society's rules having been flung out the window by the "new" Joyce Clarkson, perhaps she would perform her first blow job. Who knows what might happen? But Joyce's memory was kind of rusty, because she wasn't unzipping the old fly. So I left her boobs to dangle and did it myself. I even unbuckled my belt and pulled my pants down to my knees. And finally I leaned back and exposed myself to her, hoping to jolt the wheels of her memory back into the groove.

"David," she said, "what in the world are you doing?"

"I just thought I'd give you some help."

"You call that giving me *help?*"

"Yeah. Come on, Joyce. Look at me. Christ, I'm the goddamn Washington Monument."

"David, don't flatter yourself. Be a good boy and pull your pants back up."

"Oh, Joyce ..."

"One thing you should know," she said, suddenly jumping out of the car, "—I'm not a machine!"

She slammed the car door and ran into her house. Left sitting there with my pants down around my knees, I frantically imagined that I was playing the lead role in a biographical movie about Henry the Mo.

The next day, instead of returning to school, I decided to get a haircut. While walking around the shopping district of Bushmont Village that morning, I noticed that people were looking at me strangely. Did they know of my indiscretion with Joyce the night before? Were they whispering, "There goes David the Mo"? It was weird, because if there was ever a place I fit into, it was Bushmont. Going to the barber was a normal thing for me to do. Odd, then, how people were looking at me so strangely.

I was heading for Joe's Barber Shop. Joe had been cutting my hair from the day I had climbed out of my bassinet. To get a clipping from Joe the Barber was as natural to me as drinking milk. But then I realized why people were staring at me—my long hair! At first the sensation of being looked at, of being *frowned* upon, was unnerving. I had often wondered what it was like for a black person to walk around in the village section. Many a night I had dreamt of being discriminated against by, say, the man in the stationery store. Not that he was a bigot, or that he refused to serve black customers—I simply knew that blacks were stared at and frowned upon in our community. If only because they were so out of place.

I'd often hear people say things like, "I wonder what that colored guy is doing here." I mean, everyone knew that no blacks *lived* in Bushmont, so why would one be *shopping* in our village? Blacks, cripples, blind people—and now, presenting David Marsh with his long hair! Yes, after the first rush of embarrassment in my gut, a feeling of tremendous excitement welled up inside me. Go ahead, you housewives and storekeepers and little old ladies, stare at me!

So this was how it felt, a combination of awkwardness and anger and defiance—and how exhilarating and delicious it was! Maybe not for a *real* black person, but certainly for me. As I waited for a light at the main corner of town, two guys came by in a red car and one yelled out the window, "Hey, faggot!" For one of the few times in his life, David Marsh, the All-American boy, son of Bushmont, felt out of place and, and!—experienced personal outrage. No psychophysical exercises needed, just a long shaggy head of hair! This, I knew, was a major event. I have since wondered if my experience held a clue to the *raison d'être* of long hair. For fellows like me it produced, if only for fleeting moments, actual—not simulated!—barriers to full acceptance in society, which in turn produced a genuine experience of what it must be like to live as a black man in white America. Am I overplaying this? Perhaps, but no one had ever, or would ever, call me a "nigger" and now, for the first time, the word "faggot" had flown at me from the lips of a fast-driving, crew-cut sonofabitch from Bushmont, and to me this was an educational experience of the kind I had always sought but never found.

So I didn't get a haircut, naturally. Joe the Barber had lost a customer. I walked around town for a while longer, getting accustomed to my new role as an outcast. And here is the paradox—while I enjoyed being frowned upon by people I didn't care about, by people I didn't like anyway, I still didn't *really* want to be an outcast. Not among my own friends, anyway.

Well, I don't want to brag, but I should point out that it's just possible I really *was* ahead of my time – for 1959, at any rate. Few students appreciated my new appearance. Most figured I was either an oddball or just a sloppy guy. After a few days of walking around in school and getting laughed at, I broke down and paid a visit to Joe the Barber.

"You should have left it long," said Joyce, who had forgiven me for exposing myself to her in the car.

"My parents *forced* me to cut it," I lied.

Anyhow, we were getting back together again. On a

Saturday morning, one of the first days of spring, we took a drive up to Connecticut and had one of those "perfect days" everybody has in the movies. We got out of the car and walked through a field to see some cows. We spent the whole day doing whatever came into our heads. In one little town, we walked into an antique shop and chatted with the proprietor for almost an hour. It was really a different kind of day. I kept reminding myself that Joyce was looking for *vibrations*, so I outdid myself in the way of giggling and clowning—you know what I mean. We spent about three hours in this one town, and after a while I really *did* have the feeling that we were making a movie. A three-hour film called *David and Joyce in Connecticut*. As we walked along the sidewalk, I imitated the antique-shop proprietor. The more Joyce laughed the more I kept it up. We came across a group of little boys with a basketball and I started throwing it around with them while Joyce watched from the sidelines. Later, over a cup of coffee, she said, "You were really nice with those boys. I could see how they trusted you and looked up to you. Their faces glowed. That was really outstanding, David." Of course, baby! I have had years of practice in this sort of thing! And at the same time I was thinking that I could play the lead role in a television series about a guy who keeps moving from town to town, leaving his vibrations wherever he goes. I also thought that I was more suitable to do film acting rather than stage acting, a discovery which led me to admit, finally, that I was usually bored to death when I went to see Broadway plays with Ken Starro. The only one I had seen which had really moved me was *A Raisin in the Sun* with Sidney Poitier.

At any rate, in the weeks that followed we kept referring to "our day" in Connecticut. We even started holding hands in the high-school corridors again. The only difference in our relationship was that it had become more cerebral, if that's the word. We carried on these long discussions about individuality and personal freedom and so on. And frankly, our sex life had gone way downhill. Joyce let me kiss her and feel her up, but she had imposed a ban on any further developments. Gone were the days of the dry-hump and the cold hand between my legs! An era had passed!

One night at the Duck Inn I got up the courage to tell her, in the most civilized manner possible, that I was going out of my skull. I stopped just short of admitting that my whacking-off activities had stepped up because of her. Since she had declared that she was no longer a "machine," it had become my habit to jerk off in the car immediately after taking her home from a date. It just wasn't natural.

"All I'm trying to say," I told Joyce, "is that we don't seem to be having as much fun as we used to."

"You mean *you* aren't having as much fun," Joyce replied. "What do you mean?"

"I don't have to spell it out, David, or do I? You just want to *use* me, for your *own pleasure*. That's what you did before."

"*You* used to enjoy yourself, too," I persisted.

"Not in the way I should have," she snapped.

It's amazing how a girl can assume a powerful position so abruptly. Joyce's transformation involved more than simple appearances. At nearly eighteen, she'd become a grown woman. Her parents had been divorced after Mr. Clarkson, the TV-network big shot, had been discovered shacking up with one of his young secretaries. Even as a small child Joyce had been a strong, willful person, but now she was almost frightening.

In the plainest of words, using the most romantic of

tones, she had informed me on numerous occasions lately, "I'm not taking any more of this shit." Each time she said it I nodded my head gravely, even sympathetically. Not that I understood what all the "shit" was. I no longer felt a sense of control when I was with her. In fact, I had a vague apprehension that any moment she'd grab my hand and start swinging me around and around over her head. Why was she so annoyed, so angry at the world? I didn't really know, but I sensed that one day she might see me as *part* of that world, and in that case I'd probably have to start rebelling against my own self, however in hell you're supposed to do that.

So there we were, two teen-agers romantically sipping beer in a booth at the Duck Inn, when Joyce Clarkson calmly offered a clue to her discontent: "I'm sexually unsatisfied. I want to have an orgasm."

Without warning I felt my face become red from embarrassment. How many seventeen-year-old guys, I wondered, had received such honesty from their girlfriends? Oh, is *that* all, Joyce? I acted as if she were telling me the most normal sort of thing, as if we were discussing her desire to have a new dress for the Easter Dance.

When I didn't say anything for a few minutes, she went on: "I think it's only fair, David. If you just want sex for yourself, *you* can find a prostitute and pay for it. Or you can find a girl who doesn't mind being *used*. But if you want to have full pleasure with *me*, then *I* want it, too."

For a moment I almost expected her to produce a five-page manifesto on *Why Joyce Clarkson Wants an Orgasm*. The thing was, she was making complete sense to me. Yes, the word "equality" rang little bells of recognition in my head. So I nodded my head in full agreement, without telling her that until this very moment I had never been quite sure whether girls were *supposed* to have orgasms. Oh, I guess I knew, but I hadn't known that they *wanted* orgasms. Carefully, trying hard not to reveal my ignorance, I got Joyce to give me a crash course in some of the facts of life. For more than three hours she chattered away about the contraction of her pelvic muscles and the stimulation of her vaginal walls. I learned, for example, that she had ruptured her hymen while playing tennis at the Bushmont Beach and Yacht Club. People watching us from a distance might have thought we were discussing the play-by-play of Brookdale High's latest basketball game. Joyce's hands gestured vividly as she talked. I was showered with words such as "clitoris" and "vestibule" and "uterus." Several times I told her to *lower your voice, please.*

When we finally left the Duck Inn my brain was filled with a huge, full-color vision of Joyce's vagina. And now, Joyce, are we going to put all of this theory into practice?

"One thing," she said quite seriously. "I don't ever want to make love to you in a car again. It's degrading."

Only half-joking I said, "Can I *kiss* you in the car?"

"Of course, silly."

It was true that Joyce and I had never had intercourse. Part of the reason might have been my old Catholic training, but it was also largely because I had been quite content, in the past, to let her jerk me off. But now the clitoris had entered my life. Some guys dream of becoming lawyers or doctors or professional athletes, but me, I was consumed by an overpowering ambition to give my girlfriend an orgasm.

The whole thing was a bit too clinical for my taste, but after all, the fate of a romance seemed to be at stake. We made plans to spend a day in a motel up in the Catskill Mountains. I spent a whole afternoon working up the courage to walk into a drugstore and buy a package of condoms. I won't even go into it, it was so typical. I told the druggist that I was buying the condoms for my father. I'm sure he didn't believe me for a second. And I was so excited about getting them that I reached out and shook the druggist's hand at the conclusion of the sale.

Anyway, Joyce and I hopped in the car on a Saturday morning and headed north to the hills, where Dr. Marsh would perform his first orgasm on a human being other than himself. We had told our folks that we were going to go skiing for the day and that we'd be home around midnight. Plenty of time, I thought. Perhaps unnecessarily, we had constructed a huge network of lies to cover our tracks. Eddie Reilly might have called it Operation Orgasm.

"Intercourse," she was saying as I drove, "should not be just another form of male masturbation." Oh, Joyce, you were so quotable!

Without going into any more detail than I have to, I should indicate that Operation Orgasm was a total failure. It was one of the most dismal, frustrating days of my entire life. We got into the motel room and Joyce acted like a drill sergeant barking orders. But nothing worked. I must have ejaculated five times in all, while Joyce never even came *near* to a climax. By the time we went out for dinner I was feeling so guilty and miserable and small and weak that I nearly *crawled* along after her.

Biting into her roast beef sandwich, Joyce said, "I did have one, once."

"Had what?"

"A climax."

"You did? With me?"

"No, silly, of course not with you."

Oh, how low had I sunk?

"Then who in hell *with*?" I asked.

"With nobody," she replied. "I did it to myself. That's common among women, you know."

Boy, was my spirit depressed. I could barely eat anything. We ordered some coffee and Joyce patted me on the arm. She said, "I think it's your foreplay."

Oh, you think so, eh? Okay, Joyce, we'll go back into that goddamn motel room and I'll give you *three hours* of foreplay. All night!

And that's just about what I did, too. In fact, I foreplayed myself right into the ground. I gave her so much "preparation," as she called it, that both my arms ached and I wound up with a stiff neck.

"I'm ready!" Joyce announced suddenly. The moment had arrived! But I felt around for the object of her desire and couldn't find it!

"Hurry," Joyce said.

Where *is* it, I wondered as I felt around between my legs. Ah, *there* it is. Now the problem was to obtain an instant erection.

"What's the matter?" said Joyce.

"It's no use. I guess I'm just too tired. I can't do it."

"Oh, David. And I was so *ready!*"

"I'm sorry, Joyce. I really am."

Actually I was more than just sorry. I was angry as hell, both at myself and, perhaps more so, at Joyce.

"You tried hard, David. You really tried. And I appreciate you for that."

"It's so great," I said, putting on my clothes, "knowing how much I'm appreciated."

"Are you being sarcastic?"

"Yes."

"David, the world hasn't ended. You've just discovered that you need some more experience, that's all. We can try again some other time."

"Maybe we should stop seeing each other," I said.

"Don't be silly, David. I love you."

"Then stop treating me like a little child! Dammit, Joyce, I don't need this relationship! How am I gonna go out on stage and produce great tragic emotions if my entire brain is being lopsided by your clitoris?"

She thought that was very funny. Oh, how the girl laughed. The more she giggled, the angrier I became. On the way home from the Catskills, I drove in silence for nearly an hour.

"You think you've failed me, don't you?" said Joyce. "That's right, baby. You're the Queen of the Amazon." Which sent her into another round of hysterics. Finally she settled down again and said, "Sex isn't everything."

"Thank God."

"Seriously, David, it's really more important that we're able to *communicate* with each other."

"Yes, yes, you're undoubtedly right."

"I mean, how many other people are able to be as *honest* with each other as we are?"

"I have no idea."

"Not many, I'll bet. And it pleases me, David, that you've learned to think about *me* for a change. Now you're concerned with more than just self-gratification."

"Right, right!"

"Did you know that lots of women actually *fake* their climaxes, in order to boost the man's ego?"

"That's terrible."

"*Most* women do, I think. They go on cheating themselves just so their husbands can maintain their *image* of masculinity."

"That's really terrible, Joyce."

"What pleases me most, David, is that your *pride* isn't hurt."

"Uh hunh."

"You're *different* from most other guys, David. I've finally discovered that. You place a higher *value* on me than most guys place on their girlfriends. You've proven today that you're willing to treat me as a person and not just as a product."

"True, how true."

She kissed me on the cheek when I let her off that night at her door. Later on, in my bedroom at home, I got out some of my girlie magazines and stared at the pictures for about two hours, trying to arouse myself. Nothing happened.

The saving grace was that Joyce and I could intellectualize everything. Every morning I picked her up for school in the "short" and we had these vigorous discussions about sex and school and the theatre. In my imagination we were Joyce The Tiger and David The Impotent. Somehow, getting angry at things seemed to make up for my feelings of sexual inadequacy. I found myself lying to her a great deal, for this reason. I told her that I hated my home life and school in general, and my parents and teachers in particular. The expression of all that emotion seemed to be necessary in order to keep up with her. It was my habit to drive with my back almost against the car door, my left arm and sometimes even my head leaning out the window, which was how the cool guys drove. And when the Everly Brothers came on the radio, I nearly *hiked* out the window like you're supposed to do on a sailboat. It was all very good for the displaying of my rebellious temperament.

Even in that category, however, Joyce was way

ahead of me. In actual fact I had a very good relationship with my parents, and I didn't really hate my teachers at all. It's hard to describe accurately the feeling I had about being in senior year of high school, but it wasn't anywhere near what I made it out to be. Maybe it was a kind of quiet desperation, I don't know. For example, it didn't help any when we were told that Brookdale High was one of the best schools in the country. To begin with, that was a pretty depressing statement, because if we had the best, what were other schools like? See, the students didn't feel that Brookdale High was such a great school, not really. And if it *was* the best in the country, what did that say about the country?

But as I say, Joyce was way ahead of me. While I had these vague feelings about school, Joyce was actually getting into *fights* with her teachers and especially with the Girls' Dean. Maybe it was an extension of her continuing battles at home. The supercharged atmosphere in the Clarkson household frightened the hell out of me, always had. Following her parents' divorce, Joyce had become "older" in many ways, and now Mrs. Clarkson had a lover, a guy named Milton, who was making passes at Joyce. Very complicated, and very screwed up. Every time I picked up Joyce in the morning, she'd tell of some new argument she'd had with mother and lover.

"Right after graduation," she told me, "I'm leaving home. The *day* I graduate I'm getting out of there."

Which would compel me to drive a little faster and to pretend, actually, that I was leading her out of this living hell.

It occurred to me that perhaps I was being used, in a way. For example, one time when I was over at her house, Joyce indicated (but not directly to me) that we were going to get married right after graduation. This bit of bad news came out of her mouth during a particularly nasty argument among daughter, mother and lover. All Mrs. Clarkson said was, "Good! Get married, go on! I just hope you know what a little bitch you'd have for a wife, David."

Mrs. Clarkson was in her early forties, still quite attractive and young-looking. Milton the Lover was in his thirties, about six feet tall and very muscular. He resembled a hoodlum of sorts when he wore his T-shirt and exposed the tattoos on his arms. The dark-haired lover was involved, according to Joyce, in the high echelons of organized crime. I was a lot more worried over the fact that he was making passes at my girlfriend.

At any rate, Joyce's mother and Milton went away for a weekend in late April, and Joyce invited me over to the house in order to continue our joint pursuit of sexual liberation. "I've decided," she told me, "that I should take the *whole blame* for what happened. The trouble, David, was that I *approached* you in the wrong way."

"You did?"

"Yes. I wasn't aggressive enough, David. I should have been more *animalistic* with you."

"You think so?"

"I certainly do, and I'd like to try it out as soon as possible."

To tell the truth, I would have much preferred playing a little baseball at the Town Yard that weekend, and maybe going into the city to Madison Square Garden for a basketball game. Just about anything but sex with Joyce Clarkson!

"Listen," I said, "I'm afraid your mother might come home and catch us."

"She won't," said Joyce. "She's too busy with that dirty old man, in the first place. And besides, I don't give a damn if she *does* catch us. Maybe she'd kick me out of the house, which would be fine with me."

I had the feeling that Joyce actually *wanted* us to get caught. But I couldn't come up with a decent argument why we shouldn't make use of her empty house. Joyce had purchased a diaphragm, by the way. We snuck into her house together on Saturday afternoon, and we went upstairs to her mother's bedroom. "No reason why we shouldn't use the double bed," she informed me as she took off her clothes. I lit a cigarette and went over to the window to check for police cars and maybe even FBI men hiding behind trees. Joyce had ducked into the bathroom and now she returned, stark naked, and said, "Hurry up, silly."

I got undressed slowly, all the while trying to relay messages from my brain to my penis—please, *please* get aroused! To make a long story short, Joyce pushed me down on the double bed and proceeded to attack me according to her latest "animalistic" theory. She blew in my ear until I thought I'd lose my hearing, she sat on top of me and rolled me over and over, and worked us into several wild new "positions" she had read about. All while I remained absolutely limp, unable to obtain even a *small* erection. Once in a while Joyce would roll off me onto her back to rest, only to renew her attack with more ferocity than before. Oh, for the good old whack-off days, when life had been so simple! Finally, perhaps in desperation, Joyce decided to blow me. I lay on my back while she knelt on the floor and buried her blond head between my legs. If I don't get aroused now, I thought, my dreams of becoming a man of feeling are dashed forever! But wait! I felt the smallest beginnings of what was, to me, evidence that I just might possibly still be alive, that I hadn't been turned entirely to stone. "Keep it up, Joyce," I said as if I were at one end of a rowboat yelling for her to pull faster on the oars. "It's getting there, Joyce! Ah! Keep it up!"

Just then I happened to glance to my left. I was lying down on my back, with Joyce's head between my legs, and I glanced to my left, over my shoulder, at the door. Standing there, watching us, was Mrs. Clarkson. How *long* she had been standing there is still not known to me. At any rate, before I could react, before I could tell Joyce to stop, look up and see her mother, Mrs. Clarkson very discreetly slammed the door, jolting everything in the room including my eardrums.

Joyce looked up—she seemed so very far away down there —as if to say, What happened? I sat up quickly and said, "Your mother."

"Really?"

"Yes, really. Come on, let's get dressed."

"Screw that," she snapped, jumping up beside me on the bed. "Come on, don't bother with her."

"Are you kidding?" I yelled, sliding off the bed and pulling on my clothes. For a minute or so I considered jumping out a window. But Joyce was calmly getting dressed, almost as if she were glad to have a reason to confront her mother. We were dressed when Mrs. Clarkson knocked on the bedroom door and said, "Hurry up and get out of there."

"Don't get excited," Joyce yelled, a tremble in her voice that seemed a result of both fright and anger.

A few minutes later I followed Joyce down the stairs. Her mother was waiting in the living room. "David," said Mrs. Clarkson, "I don't ever want to see you in this house again. I don't even want to catch you *talking* to my daughter again. You understand?"

Before I could answer, Joyce said, "He doesn't

understand anything of the kind!"

"Go out through the kitchen door," Mrs. Clarkson yelled at me. "I don't even want to see you!"

"What are you so upset about?" Joyce yelled at her mother. "You've been living with that creep of a lover for the past five months! What makes David any worse than Milton?"

"Shut up!"

I went into the kitchen while they argued. As long as I could remember, the Clarkson household had been charged with a highly volatile atmosphere. Which was just the opposite from the way things were done in my house, where a raised voice was looked upon as a major event in life. Milton the Lover was sitting at the kitchen table, drinking a beer. In the other room, Joyce and her mother were on the verge of throwing furniture at each other. Smiling at me, Milton said, "You really put it to her, eh?"

15

Moving On

It came as a big shock to everybody, including me, when I didn't get accepted to any of the colleges of my choice. Was it possible that a good Catholic boy like me could be turned away by Notre Dame, Georgetown *and* Villanova? "There must be a mistake," said my father, but a subsequent investigation proved that there wasn't. A visitor would have thought there had been a death in the family, the way my folks took the good news. Yes, *good* news, because privately I was glad. A faint rumble of excitement was beginning inside me—was it too much to hope for, to be set adrift in America without a college degree? That, it seemed, was the essence of Hard Times. Was I actually going to have the opportunity to go off on my own, unconnected with any institution of learning or living, and *flounder*?

"What I'd like to do," I told Neil, "is to go to New York City and maybe live at the YMCA or in some small room in Greenwich Village. I won't even try to get an acting job, not for five or even ten years. Instead, I'll go to a good acting school, one where they teach the Method, and do odd jobs to maintain my existence."

Man, was I excited about not getting into college. As far as I was concerned, it was the greatest thing that ever happened to me. "Neil," I said one afternoon as we walked to the school parking lot, "it seems that everything in my life, from birth onward, has conspired to drain me of whatever chance to *live* that I might possess. And now, it looks as if I'm gonna get that chance, after all."

"I don't get it," he said. "I always figured you *wanted* to go to college."

"Shit, no," I said. "I was *resigned* to going, that's all. But see, there's a *fundamental problem* to be solved. I've got to jump out of the framework of the life that I'm in, and create a whole *new* one."

"You can't change who you are, David. You're gonna be *eighteen* this year. If you were John Keats, you'd have less than nine years to live! You've been conditioned along certain lines. Your only hope is to die and be reincarnated, which shouldn't be ruled out."

"Big help," I replied. "See, you don't understand what I mean. I'm gonna establish a whole new *background*, Neil. I'm gonna completely wipe away the Bushmont aspect of my experience and put a new one in its place."

"It is true," noted the Mad Philosopher with great care, "that environment is a primary factor in the development of a person's character."

"Right, Neil! I'm gonna change my environment! And if I live in the new environment long enough, it'll change my character! And *then* I'll go try to get jobs as an actor."

Ah, but I should have known better. In May my father and mother drove us up to a little place in New England called Cosgrove College. It was supposed to have a drama department with a real good reputation, whatever that meant. I think it meant that one of my mother's friends from the Women's Club, who had graduated from Cosgrove College as a speech major in 1936, was now Chairman of the Holy Family Pageant Committee, which put on a religious playlet every Christmas. We went up there in the car and checked it out, and Dad brought me right over to the administration building to fill out an application. Then we headed for the Drama Department, so I tried to adopt a James Dean shuffle and a Marlon Brando mumble. It was pretty difficult to sustain, since I was wearing a stupid green-plaid sports jacket and white bucks. No, I didn't look like perfect material for the lead role in *On the Waterfront.*

Anyway, I had an interview with Mr. Blomsky, who was head of the Cosgrove Drama Department. He seemed to know a lot about the theatre, although I didn't think to ask him why he was wasting all that talent in the hills of New England. But then he mentioned Stanislavski and the Method, and I was sucked right in. We took a walk backstage, where some students were rehearsing for a one-act play. They all had very resonant voices. Their nasality was very good. But their acting was unbelievably wooden and without emotion.

Mr. Blomsky went back into his office and he said, "Have you ever heard of Norman Merriweather?"

"Uh ...."

"Oh, you *must* have heard about Norman Merriweather."

"Yeah, well ..."

"He graduated from here," Mr. Blomsky said, smiling. Oh, fine! Terrific!

So I was accepted at Cosgrove College, right then and there. We went back to the Dean's Office and the whole thing was settled.

On the way home I said, "Dad, have you ever heard of Norman Merriweather?"

"Who?"

Yeah, that's what I wondered. I went to the Bushmont Library a few days later and looked through all the anthologies of movie actors and stage performers and whatnot. But not a trace of Norman Merriweather. What had become of this Cosgrove graduate who had brought such a glow into Mr. Blomsky's heart? Was he a spear-carrier in the movie version of *The Robe?* Was his the actual voice for Donald Duck? Norman Merriweather! God knows who he was, but I was heading off into the sunset and following in his footsteps, wherever they led.

At about the same time, Eddie Reilly was told that his marks were so low he'd have to repeat senior year of high school. He wasn't going to graduate with the rest of us. How I found out was that his mother had told my mother, and Mom told me. I can't say that I was too surprised, but I did find myself becoming terribly sad and even angry about it. Hadn't Eddie Reilly made some beautiful cabinets and other things out of wood in his shop class? Eddie also had taken up photography. He took photographs of people and developed them in his cellar. And he had become a terrific grease monkey at a local gas station in his spare time. Nobody could take apart and put together an engine the way he could. And hadn't he learned so much from people in general, like Mr. Greene and countless others? So why was I getting a diploma while he wasn't? What kind of justice was that?

I went over to his house one evening after dinner, wondering what his reaction to being "left back" in school had been. Would he be as angry and indignant about it as I was? Or would he be glad, or what?

He was playing a game of chess with his father in the den next to their living room. I had forgotten that Dr. Reilly was a big chess player, and that Eddie had learned the game for his father's benefit. The two of them were on opposite sides of a small table, staring down at the board. I said a big hello but neither of them answered or even looked up. In the silence I sat down to watch.

One thing about Dr. Reilly, he was like a little kid

sometimes. The smallest things could make him laugh so hard that tears came into his eyes. As I've mentioned, long ago his medical colleagues had told him that he'd never even be able to walk because of the multiple sclerosis or Parkinson's disease or whatever, but he'd maintained his general practice ever since then, almost as if to prove a point. The guy could barely control his body, yet he drove a car and visited all kinds of patients who weren't anywhere near as disabled as he was. Maybe that's why he appreciated so many little things, like going to get his shoes polished. I used to join Eddie and him when they went to the shoe store in Bushmont. Eddie would help him onto the chair and set his feet in place, and you've never seen a grown man so pleased about having his shoes shined. This was like an *event* in his life. Sitting up there on the shoeshine stand, for him, was the way it is for a small child to go up in an airplane or in one of the rides at Playland.

Dr. Reilly carefully moved a chess piece and sat back, grinning from ear to ear. He had white hair, and his face got red when he tried to stifle his enjoyment of something. Eddie moved a piece, and Dr. Reilly's face became serious again. This went on for about an hour, a really intense competition between father and son. And then something strange happened. I didn't know that much about chess, but I had a feeling that Eddie suddenly relaxed, that he moved a piece without being quite as careful as before. And I think he did it on purpose. Dr. Reilly's face was getting red again, redder than all the other times, and he came in for the kill.

"*Haaaaaaa!*" he shouted in triumph, moving a piece so that Eddie was trapped. My friend just sat there, shaking his head in defeat. Had he lost the game on purpose? I couldn't tell by his face.

"Well," he said under his breath, "can't win 'em all."

Eddie then pulled the table away from his father and went around to help him out of his chair. When Dr. Reilly sat still for long periods of time, his muscles seemed to stiffen. Eddie held his arm out and literally had to pull Dr. Reilly to his feet. The old man (he really wasn't that old, but he looked it) wavered a bit, trying to capture his balance. Eddie stood next to him, waiting to help him across the living room to the stair landing. Dr. Reilly waved him away, however, saying, "I can do it." When he spoke it sounded as if he were drunk, because the illness apparently had affected his speech. "I'm fine," he said almost to himself. "I'm just fine."

Eddie started putting away the chess pieces, his back to his father, who was still wavering from side to side. Suddenly Dr. Reilly started across the living room. He sort of tilted the top half of his body forward, to get himself moving. And in order to prevent himself from falling on his face, he worked his rubbery legs one after another in a race with gravity. *Thump, thump, thump, thump* he went across the room, crashing into the bannister at the bottom of the stairs. All this time, Eddie did not turn around to watch. He slowly put the chess pieces into a box, but I could tell he was holding his breath.

After a moment Eddie turned and called, "Can I help you up the stairs, Dad?"

"No," came Dr. Reilly's slurred speech. "I'm all right."

Eddie slumped down on the couch and picked up a magazine. I was still sitting in my chair, but I didn't try to start a conversation yet. Dr. Reilly was going up the stairs, one by one. He had to pull himself, holding the bannister, up each of the fourteen steps. I knew there were fourteen, because I had heard Mrs. Reilly mention it one time.

We listened as Eddie's father lifted one leg and then another, a process that took, altogether, more than fifteen minutes. How in hell did he ever drive that car? How did he get his foot to the brake in time? How did he get himself dressed and undressed? When he got to the top of the stairs, I figured it was only a matter of a few moments until he fell backwards down the whole flight to the bottom. I kept waiting for the crash. The last three or four steps were almost unbearable. I watched Eddie's face—behind that calm expression he, too, was waiting for the worst.

When we heard Dr. Reilly thumping down the upstairs hallway—again with a crash when he came to a halt—we both seemed to take a long breath of air. And I suddenly realized that Eddie went through this kind of thing almost every night of his life. Once was enough for me, but *every night?* And what about when his father came *down* the stairs? Or when he went out of the house? I had never realized this one aspect of Eddie's life. I had known about it, maybe, but I hadn't ever *felt* it.

"Hey," said Eddie. "Want a beer?"

"Sure."

We went downstairs to his cellar and played some pool while we drank the beer. Eddie's model trains were still set up in half of the basement, sitting there under several layers of dust.

"Your father," I said, "he's really something. When did he get his illness? At birth, or what?"

"Nah. He was maybe twenty-five or so."

"How'd it happen, Ed?"

"It just did, all of a sudden. It was like he lost control, right out of the blue."

For the first time, it occurred to me that Eddie might be afraid that the same thing would happen to him some day. Was he living in constant fear of being physically slowed down like his father? Of maybe being confined to a chair or even a bed for the rest of his life?

"I heard about you being left back in school," I said.

"Yeah."

"I'm sorry to hear that, Ed. Jeez, you must have a lot of bastards for teachers."

"Yeah, well, school is school. I'd rather learn by doing something, anyway."

"Are you gonna really have to repeat the whole senior year?"

"I dunno. I may just quit."

"Without a diploma?"

"I dunno. Maybe."

"Are you still going away?"

"Maybe. I dunno."

"I always figured it was definite, Ed."

"Yeah, but my father's getting worse, although he doesn't know it. I might have to stick around, I dunno."

"What'll you do?"

"I dunno."

"Well, Ed, you'll think of something."

"Yeah."

"You really should finish high school first, though."

"Then I'll probably have to go in the Army or something."

"Oh, yeah, I didn't think about that."

"You don't have to, Dave."

I looked at my good friend, standing there with his pool stick, and I suddenly had the feeling that things were closing in on him. Weird, too, how he did, in fact, resemble James Dean. But the strangest thing of all, I didn't envy him.

I'd rather learn by doing something.

Had Eddie Reilly said that? Had he actually put into words something of what made him, to me at least, a special person? Had he given a clue? See, I may not have envied the guy—I never really envied him, in fact—but I sure as hell *admired* him. In appearance, in behavior, in the way he seemed to attract other people to him, in *form* if not in content, I had always wanted to be like Eddie. *Learn by doing.* Maybe, I thought, that was part of his secret. And maybe that was why he'd never been able to adjust to school of any kind. In school, you hardly ever learned by doing anything. You listened and thought and *studied* things, but very seldom did you *do* something in order to learn it. And only by doing things, by *acting* (ahhhhh!), did a person acquire knowledge in an emotional and personal way. No wonder he hated school!

Still, I was glad to graduate from Brookdale High at last. I had heard some talk that Eddie might go to some prep school in upstate New York in order to get his diploma. Lots of dumb guys from wealthy families did that, but mainly in order to get into a decent college. I found it hard to believe that Eddie (whose folks weren't rich by any means) might consent to it, though. Why didn't everybody just leave him alone?

I found out that he was working on a fishing boat for the summer. It was one of those boats that took out "fishing parties" every morning from Brookdale Harbor. My father used to take me on them when I was maybe twelve or thirteen. We'd get on the boat with some other landlubbers and go out into the middle of

Long Island Sound to fish for flounders or whatever was running. The captain always had a couple of helpers on board, to drop the anchor and assist us with our bait and tackle. And so Eddie was learning by doing! In a very short time my friend would *become a fisherman,* and then he'd drop the whole thing and take up another activity like bartending or gardening or whatever. In fact, what he was doing—what he did all the time, as a way of life!—was exactly what I needed to be doing in order to become a good actor. He was involving himself in life! Ahhhh!

I started looking through the classified ads of our local paper, and I wound up getting a job driving an ice-cream truck. It was sort of a poor man's Good Humor truck, almost a wagon on four wheels. I was going to *become a Popsicle Man!* Not quite as romantic as being a helper on a fishing boat, but still, I was pretty damn excited. People would ask me what I was doing for the summer and I'd say, "Truck-driver," without mentioning the Popsicle aspect of it. Part of my truck route included the Flats, and I'd sort of drive through it in a hurry. As I've mentioned, I had always thought of the Flats as a pretty violent and terrible place. But it's funny, because I began to like it. The Flats seemed much more alive than the Village of Bushmont. I enjoyed seeing all kinds of people walking around, even if they did seem grubby and poor.

And the people seemed to look forward to my arrival, too, as if I were an oddity, which I was. I'd come rolling down a narrow cobblestone street with old shabby houses on either side, sitting there in my white suit and jangling those stupid bells—and I guess I probably did look kind of odd.

Once in a while I'd become afraid, though. I had

heard stories about Popsicle Men being held up in the Flats, sort of like the old train robberies you'd see in the Westerns. One of my colleagues in the Popsicle trade, an elderly man, had dozens of hair-raising and even funny stories to tell. Toward the middle of the summer, though, I actually learned to *enjoy* being afraid. Either they'll overturn the truck and burn it, I thought, or they'll think I'm Billy Budd and shower me with affection.

One evening I pulled up the truck next to the ball field in the Flats, near a couple of old brick public-housing projects which had been built shortly after World War II for the G.I.'s. Now they were filled completely with black families. There was a baseball game going on between two Little League teams from the Flats. Of the players on the field, all were black except for about six or seven. I parked the truck and started ringing my goddamn bells. God knows why I hated those bells so much. Maybe they reminded me of church, I don't know. Anyhow, it also seemed somewhat perverse to be ringing the bells, because I wasn't really sure that I wanted to attract a great deal of attention. "If I can only get in and get out again, unharmed," I told myself, "then I'll feel okay."

The bleacher section was packed with black kids. I started thinking that here was a pretty good chance to sell a lot of Popsicles. The old capitalist glands were churning. But the kids just kept playing the baseball game, and cheering, as though I weren't even there. Although it was evening, the temperature was still up around eighty degrees. I couldn't figure out why nobody wanted any Popsicles.

Finally this one little boy came up to the truck and just stood there looking at the pictures of the different kinds of Popsicles and stuff. "Can I help you?" I said. "Which one would you like?"

The little boy thought a moment and then pointed to a grape-flavored Popsicle. A sale! I reached into the truck and gave him one. "That'll be ten cents," I announced.

The kid peeled off the paper and began licking his Popsicle. He refused to look me in the eye.

"Ten cents," I repeated.

"Ain't got no ten cents."

"You don't?"

"Nope."

"Then what'cha got?"

"Nothing."

"You don't have any money?"

"Nope."

"Then what did you buy one for?"

The kid just stood his ground, defiantly licking his Popsicle. I almost grabbed it back from him. IGNORANT WHITE BASTARD FROM BUSHMONT TANTALIZES, THEN TORTURES, BLACK GHETTO CHILD.

"Well," I said at last, "you might as well keep it."

"Thanks, Mister."

The kid walked away to the bleachers, but soon three of his friends came sauntering over to the truck. "All right, guys," I said. "What'll you have?" They each pointed to a different type of Popsicle. "Hey, wait a minute," I said. "You guys got money?"

"Nope," said the tallest of the three kids.

"Well, they cost ten cents apiece. Sorry."

"You gave Albert a free one."

"Yeah, and *we* ain't got any money either."

"Come on, Mister."

"Yeah, be a sport."

Spontaneously both my hands went up in the air. I held my arms outstretched, uncannily feeling like Jesus Christ about to perform a miracle. I'm not sure what emotions were going through me, not exactly, but there I was with a whole truck full of Popsicles, and it was hot outside, and the kids hadn't any money. It seemed wrong to come by with all those goodies only to make the kids remember what they didn't have. I mean, I didn't want to be like one of those phony medicine men who went out West to cheat the Indians. So, I took out three Popsicles and gave them to the kids. They raced back to the bleachers and soon a whole bunch of boys and girls came running up to the truck.

"Does anybody have any money?" I shouted like a first-class idiot.

"No!" came the chorus.

"Well, then," I replied, basking in the glory of my own generous, compassionate nature. "Step right up, wait your turn!"

Before long a gigantic crowd of black kids was waiting in line, and I was reaching inside my truck and handing out free Popsicles as fast as I could. Even the baseball players stopped and came over. I must have given away about two hundred Popsicles. At any rate, the truck was completely empty when I left the ball field, and I had this great feeling that finally I'd *done* something that summer. Something *meaningful*. Where was the photographer from the local paper? Yes, I was very self-satisfied, very righteous! I was even indignant when my boss fired me!

In fact, you might say that I inflated this incident into a major civil-rights event. "Do you understand what I did?" I screamed at my mother and father. "Do you have the faintest notion of the *significance* of what I did?"

"Next you'll want to give our house away," my father said. I couldn't tell whether he was joking or not, but for a few minutes I actually considered it as a real possibility.

Joyce Clarkson was planning to go to college in Florida, mainly so she could play tennis and water ski, I think. As she explained to me, "I am a physical, as opposed to a mental, kind of person." She and I sat on the beach down at the Club a lot during the rest of that summer. She'd be rolling over at various intervals in order to keep an even tan, and adjusting her transistorized radio at intervals in order to keep a steady flow of music, while I carefully pored through Harold Clurman's book, *The Fervent Years*.

I think I was nostalgic about a past already, before even acquiring one of my own. There was something about the 1930s that attracted the hell out of me. The word "fervent" sent chills up and down the sides of my head and made water suddenly spring up in my eyes. The Group Theatre! Maybe it was the image of all those people working together in a personal way, for a single, collective goal, that got to me. For a guy who was born in 1941, I was pretty damn nostalgic over the thirties.

There was a distinct *religious* overtone to Clurman's account of the Group Theatre. He wrote that he had wanted a play "to affect men's hearts, to change their very lives in matters of aspiration, sentiment, conviction." A play should "make men more truly alive." The theatre was a "temple" and art was a "communion." Right, Harold baby! "At each performance in the theatre," he wrote, "something happened between contemporaries that was a deep pleasure for those who loved the human vibration of people in their common play and enthusiasm."

I thought of my childhood with Eddie Reilly, the carnivals in his backyard.

"I clamored for greater occasions," Clurman wrote, "for closer embrace, for a more rooted togetherness."

So do I, Harold! So do I!

"From consideration of acting and plays, we were plunged into a chaos of life questions, with the desire and hope of making possible some new order and integration. From an experiment in the theatre we were in some way impelled to an experiment in living."

Such words gave me an ache in my stomach and produced a strange dizziness of the head. Was it possible that I might miss out on such a wondrous, moving experiment? Sitting there on the sand with Joyce Clarkson, was life going to pass right by? The ache and the dizziness seemed to twist together into a whirlpool of sinking panic.

The Group Theatre's rehearsal system was all-important. It was based upon the Stanislavski Method, utilizing improvisations and the recollection of past feelings.

"Here at last was a key to that elusive ingredient of the stage, true emotion."

Ah, yes!

The effect on the actors was "that of a miracle." It was something new and basic, "something almost holy."

Miracles! Holy! For Christ's sake, everybody, hadn't I grown up with those words thrown at me all the time?

"The actors not only rehearsed morning, noon and night, but they went swimming in a near-by pool, played, kidded, fell in love."

They did? Really?

"Everything was keyed high."

Out of this world, Mr. Clurman!

"Here was companionship, security, work, and dreams."

Oh, Jesus, Mary, and Joseph!

One night I woke up in a sweat and shouted, "That's it!"

"Are you all right?" my mother called.

"I've got an idea!"

"A what?"

"An idea! A plan! A brilliant new plan!"

"David," came my father's groggy voice, "will you please go back to sleep?"

Naturally I didn't do any such thing. I shut my door, turned on the light, and paced around a bit. Of course! Why not! I can start a Group Theatre of my own! The Bushmont Art Theatre! The Valley Stream Players! The Stinkers Present!

It seemed so simple and obvious that I wondered why I hadn't thought of it before. I could get a whole bunch of kids together—five or six, or a dozen or two dozen, *hundreds*, even—and form a Little Theatre of my own. Of *our* own, rather. A *group* effort. I'd get Eddie and Neil and Kenny and Joyce, and I'd approach all the kids in Brookdale High's drama department, all the thespians— surely they would want to join me. This would be the perfect alternative to going to college or getting a job somewhere. We could wear old clothes and support ourselves by going around the community asking for donations in the form of food and materials and small amounts of money. We'd feel very close to each other. Yes, yes! We'd find a piece of land somewhere in the Village, some empty municipal lot that nobody cares about, and we could build some sort of cabin or tent or whatever, to live in. And then, working together, we'd build our own Little Theatre. From scratch! Just a simple little building with a stage and maybe fifty seats. An intimate little place, maybe even an arena stage—a bare floor with fold-up chairs placed around it in a circle. If we did well over a period of, say, three years, maybe we'd have the money and prestige to build an even better Little Theatre, a permanent one!

If I remember correctly, I spent about three hours of

the early morning, while my folks were still asleep, writing my thoughts down in a notebook. For the next several days the idea grew in my mind until I thought of it not just as an idea but as a real possibility, almost a reality. In essence, we would create a new family, a new community, one in which we all would share the same vision. Just what vision that was, I couldn't pin down in my mind, but it didn't seem to matter at the moment. Everyone would be an equal partner in the Little Theatre, both girls and boys, and our work would be inseparable from our lives. A whole new life-style that merged working and playing, artistic creation and actual love! And, very important, the new "community" would include all races and colors and creeds. God, it sounded as if I were writing the Constitution all over again. Money would be functional, nothing more, because our basic value would be the joy of life itself. Perhaps we would also form some sort of new religion, a religion of sharing and loving. Not a day or night would pass without a torrent of laughing and crying over the beauty of being together and being ourselves! Some of us might even get married — we'd perform our own ceremonies! — and we'd raise the children in a special playground, and teach them in special schools, schools relying on experience much more than on books.

In my daydreams I imagined how all the grown-ups (and Yankee fans of whatever age) would come to watch our plays. All the dull people would sit around and watch something that would bring them back to life again. Little by little, as more people came into our theatre and out, we'd change the entire population. I had read something by Tennessee Williams which seemed to go along with my plan. He wrote about a community-theater group which was sort of "a longhaired outfit." Even though they put on bad shows, he wrote, "they never put on a show that didn't deliver a punch to the solar plexus, maybe not in the first act, maybe not in the second, but always at last a good hard punch was delivered, and it made a difference in the lives of the spectators that they had come to that place and seen that show." Right, Mr. Williams! That's it! We'd become a real *factor* in the total community! A driving force for change, to make a difference!

I sensed only in a vague way that in addition to shocking our spectators emotionally, we would have to develop some strong *ideas* as well. Clurman had noted that in the thirties "the demands of the spirit for the young people could only be satisfied by action that in some way became social and political." I had no idea what he was talking about, not really, but I figured that my group should become social and political, too. Yes, Clurman spoke of the young people's "appetite for meetings, collections, demonstrations, petitions, and parades on behalf of some cause in which a specific social issue was at stake." If only, I thought, we could look back one day on our *own* fervent years! But what kind of plays would we produce? Joyce could come out on stage and do a monologue on the need for female orgasms, maybe. In a pinch, we could always revive *Waiting For Lefty* (in Bushmont?). Or maybe, in the final analysis, we could all run out on stage and cry and scream and yell at the audience, and maybe then become real quiet and take off our clothes and make love to each other. And invite the audience to participate! Ah, but my brain was getting a little foggy on all this, so I put off the details and just daydreamed about it while lying on the beach.

A few days before I went off to Cosgrove College,

our maid, Ella Washington, had a heart attack and died. My parents and I went to her funeral. There were maybe two dozen people there, all of them black except for the three of us. Her son George was there, of course, all dressed up in a black suit and tie, looking already like a determined young lawyer. I think he had gotten a scholarship to a very good college on the West Coast.

We went to this tiny church in the Flats where they held the service for Ella. There was some terrific emotional singing by a bunch of black girls, and a long, passionate speech was given by the black minister. The whole thing was very moving. I think I almost cried for the first time in years. Afterward I shook hands with George and told him how sorry I was about his mother, my maid.

On the way home, I thought how my own church, Holy Family, seemed absolutely dead in comparison to what I had just seen. And I also thought how the church service had achieved precisely the effect on *me* that I had envisioned *my* own Group Theatre having on all the dull people in Bushmont. It seemed as if I was always winding up as a spectator.

Epilogue: 1970

Well, I won't go into the whole story of my life from 1960 to 1970. I suppose I could tell about how I went through four years of college and then lived in New York City as a young struggling actor. (At one point I had to go back up to Bushmont for a military physical, and it turned out I was 4F because of a head injury back when I was seven and ran into a gardening truck; when I got home from the hospital, families collected money to buy us a small black-and-white TV set, which became one of the first in our neighborhood.) I could tell a lot of stories about going to acting school in Greenwich Village and making the rounds of casting offices, and about how I later went into social work for a time. Then I became sort of a traveling radical, protesting against war and racism and, naturally, rooting for the New York Mets. I even spent a little time with drugs in California and did some panhandling, wearing an old Army jacket I had picked up somewhere.

Joyce and I saw each other off and on during the 1960s. We even marched in a demonstration together in Washington, D.C. Not that any of this changed me in any fundamental way, understand. In fact, Joyce and I are getting married soon, and we've got an apartment all lined up in Bronxville, New York, a place very similar to Bushmont Village. We have many interests in common, see, like going to all the latest movies in New York. And we plan to be a very mobile and involved young couple. I might add that I have been described in some circles as having "rugged, shaggy-haired good looks" and a "cool, stylish assurance."

As for Eddie Reilly, I haven't seen or heard from him in a while. I've run into him occasionally when I've gone back home to Bushmont to see the folks. Eddie had quit high school and had gone into the military for two or three years. He had gone over to Vietnam and there was some talk he came home and spent some time in an "institution" of one kind or another, but I'm not sure of that. The last time I saw him was in a little tavern in Brookdale. He had become very pale and nervous. He chain-smoked and his hands shook when he lit a match. He was nearly stone-drunk at the time, and it looked as if he hadn't gotten any sleep for several days. He said something about how he was living with a girl, or woman, and her three kids. He wasn't a "hippie" or anything like that, nor did he seem angry. I think he was just generally sad, and lost. We didn't have too much to say to each other, except the vague fact that somehow we could've been gone, whatever that meant. Eddie said he had a job as a construction worker in Brookdale, and he became excited when he described some plans he had for starting a small furniture business of his own. "I'm gonna make most of the stuff by hand," he said. "But first, I've gotta save some money." I told him I had gotten on television once during a demonstration. The camera caught me with my fist in the air as I was shouting, "Power to the People." You should have heard Eddie laugh over that one. He still had the greatest little chuckle I've heard anywhere.